THE WEDDING TRIO

DAISY LANDISH

Editing by Rachael Lammie
Cover by Daisy Landish

BEACHES AND TRAILS
PUBLISHING

About the Author

Daisy Landish is a romance and contemporary fiction author living in the UK, whose clean and sweet novellas have tugged at readers' heart-strings across the pond and beyond. When she's not writing love stories, Daisy spends her time reading, hiking at dawn, and riding into the sunset on her horse, Rosebud.

Join Daisy's Newsletter for updates and giveaways!

facebook.com/daisylandishromance

twitter.com/daisy_landish

instagram.com/beachesandtrailspublishing

amazon.com/author/daisylandish

bookbub.com/authors/daisy-landish

goodreads.com/Daisy_Landish

Also by Daisy Landish

Clean Regency Romance

The Lady Series - The Allington Collection

The Lady Series - The Gillingham Collection

The Lady Series - The Blackmore Collection

Clean Contemporary Romance

Love on Spruce Island

Second Chance

Cherry Tree Island

The Wedding Trio

The Science Fair Trilogy

Clean Contemporary Western Romance

Counting on a Cowboy

Focusing on the Cowboy

Cozy Mysteries

Jane and Kennedy Daniels Mysteries

Pine Grove Mysteries

Annie Archer Paranormal Mysteries

Wilma Wade Holiday Mysteries

Mike and Maddie Mysteries

Clean Holiday Romance

The Yuletide Thief

Grounded at Christmas

Clueless at Christmas

Christmas Surprise

Something New

THE WEDDING TRIO BOOK 1

$O_{n\varepsilon}$

JULIETTE HELD BACK the tears that she so desperately wanted to let flow. Instead, she repeated the mantra in her head: *I must stay strong for Milo.* Thinking of her son was the only way she would make it through the day. As each person came to her with tear-filled eyes and offered their condolences, she felt her heart grow with love and warmth. It wasn't the well wishes, the apologies, or the kind words of support that mattered so much. It was the love they showed to honour her beloved. *He never knew how much he was loved. The lives he touched. Oh, how I wish he knew.*

"It's going to be alright," and "We are here if you need anything," they said. Juliette knew they meant well, but their words rang hollow. *How was anything ever going to be OK? Would these people help her raise her son every day?* Her mind raced, and her heart pounded. She felt her hands tremble as she repeated her mantra. *I must stay strong for Milo.*

Old friends, college buddies, work colleagues, and distant relatives. The sea of people seemed endless. She squared her shoulders and held her head high, trying not to crumble as she retold the heartbreak of her husband's sudden departure. She wished they would stop asking. But she knew they grieved too, and needed closure, almost as much as she did.

"I need you to be the best wife and mother. Can you do that for me?" he had asked one day.

"Of course. But honey, where is this coming from? Is everything OK?" She'd worried when he'd asked the question seemingly out of the blue.

She remembered how he'd smiled sweetly at her, brushing her hair out of her eyes. "Everything is fine. A man just likes to hear his lady make a promise every once in a while."

Had he known he was dying? She asked herself that constantly. She cursed herself for not prying further. Her gut had told her his question was odd, but she trusted him and let her concerns go. With her husband's words in her mind, she repeated her mantra. She looked over at her son, who was wrapped tightly in his cousin's arms.

She had always been an independent woman, even before her marriage. And she planned to not let herself, her son, or her story slip into a place of pity. She appreciated the kind words of others.

There were even a few she knew would follow through in their promise to be there. But she didn't intend to rely on anyone else. Nor did she want to. She needed to adjust to the life of a widow. It was a life that she hadn't expected to have so young.

The rest of the day played out in a blur. She gave her eulogy. She listened to others speak, but couldn't recount a single word. *Fourteen, Milo is only fourteen. That's too young for a son to lose his father.* These thoughts would not leave her alone.

She worried for Milo. He had been so close to his father. They did everything together. Best friends. It was a beautiful bond. She worried how Milo would carry on without his other half. She hoped she could be enough for him.

She played back the moment she got the call. He had passed while at work, a heart attack. *But at least he wasn't alone*, she told herself to try and bring herself some comfort.

"Did he know he was sick? Had he shown any signs? I would call his doctor and find out. He obviously was keeping something from you. What if it's hereditary? Think of Milo." Her mother rambled beside her. The tone was critical and harsh.

"I am thinking of Milo. Milo never leaves my mind. What good will questioning anything do? Will it bring him back? No! So, leave it alone." Juliette snapped in hushed tones.

Her mother had always been a difficult woman. Juliette didn't have the energy to deal with her while she was in the process of burying her husband.

People shared stories at the wake to celebrate the life they all mourned. Juliette smiled and laughed, listening to them all. Love filled the room, wrapping around Juliette. But as she looked over to Milo, her heart ached. A light had been extinguished from his eyes. They no longer sparkled the same way. When he spoke of his father, there was no smile, just streams of tears. She wished she could take away his pain.

"Can we go home, Mom?" Milo asked as the mourners began to disperse.

"Sure, sweetie, let me just say goodbye to your Grandma," she said, kissing her son's forehead.

She bid farewell to everyone who remained and left her parent's house before heading home. Home. No. She was going to her house. Home is where the heart is. How could she call that structure home when her heart was no longer there? James had been her heart, the air she breathed, the sun in the sky.

"I'm going to bed," Milo said as he left the car and headed up the driveway to the big pale blue door.

"Do you want anything to eat? I haven't seen you eat all day," Juliette called after him, frowning with worry.

"No, thanks. I just want to sleep," he said.

Juliette went to the kitchen, to make herself a mint and jasmine tea to try and help her relax. Silence had never been so deafening. The house seemed darker. Even with her son upstairs, she had never felt so alone.

Safe in the knowledge that her son slept, she crept up to bed and finally allowed her tears to fall after turning on the shower in her en suite bathroom. She hoped the sound would hide her wails. She didn't want Milo to see her like that.

Juliette had always been strong. James had been the only person she allowed herself to be vulnerable with. So, as the weeks turned to months, she settled into a comfortable routine of crying alone in her room. They say time heals all wounds, but Juliette felt the sting of this wound growing worse with each passing day. Her grief was crushing. On the night of her wedding anniversary, she curled up on the bathroom floor holding the tie James had worn when he'd proposed. She clung to it so tight that her knuckles turned white.

She didn't hear Milo walk in, being too lost in her grief. He simply curled up next to her and wrapped her in his arms. She wanted to protest, to tell him it was her responsibility to be strong for him. But as she saw James in her son's eyes, she clung to him and sobbed.

The next morning, at breakfast, she had to say something.

She smiled weakly, not sure how to broach this conversation. "I'm so sorry you had to see me like that. It's not your responsibility to take care of me. But thank you."

"I had heard you cry a few times. The shower isn't as loud as you think. But last night, I couldn't leave you. You are my Mom. Dad would want me to protect you," Milo said without looking up from his cereal.

She had never been prouder of her son. She and James had raised him right. Lately, the more she looked at Milo, the more of James she saw.

The pain was still there as another month passed, but the tears spilled less often over time. Slowly, Juliette slipped back into a somewhat normal and comfortable life. Adjusting was still hard, but she was starting to manage everything better. Milo had even begun to smile again. She focused a lot of her energy on Milo. While it was sweet that he wanted to care for her, she was the parent, and he was still quite young. He had been through enough already. He also showed great concern for his grieving mother. The loss of her life partner left a hole that needed to be filled. He also thought that she wasn't coping as well with stressful situations as she could, understandably so.

To occupy her mind, she sat one evening and wrote down all the things that James and Milo loved to do together, along with the things she loved doing with her late husband. She wanted to keep a part of him in her life. James loved cooking and trying out new restaurants. He liked to judge who made a particular dish best, and then he would recreate it and try to make it better. He also loved weddings. His catchphrase was "I love, love." He had been a hopeless romantic. It was one of the things she loved most about him. Their marriage felt like that of a movie or fairy tale. Her friends often commented that their love was a "couple's dream." James would often tell her how she was the best thing to ever happen to him, and how happy she made him.

It sparked a flurry of joy in her chest, remembering their times together. All the sweet words he would whisper, all the kind gestures and thoughtful ways he would show her he cared.

Butterflies flurried in her stomach as she remembered their wedding day. The gleam in his eyes when he'd seen her in her wedding dress for the first time. How he cried as she walked down the aisle towards him. She knew that no one could make her feel the way James had. What they'd had was rare. A genuine diamond. True love romance.

Juliette smiled at all the memories she had made with her husband. And how she would give up a lot to have that all over again.

She needed something in her life that would give her purpose again. But it had to be something that could remind her every day of the love she was blessed to share. She ripped her list from the page and wrote a pros and cons list. First, she started with the idea of opening a restaurant. *James was the foodie, not me.* Then, ripping out the page to start again, her eyes fell on her wedding ring.

"You're rushing into things. Take your time. Slow down. You haven't grieved properly." How many times had everyone said these things to her lately?

Who are they to say what the right way to grieve is? I'm doing what is right for me, she told herself. Then, looking up at the picture on the dresser of her wedding day, she took a deep, soothing breath and set the pad aside.

It had been almost a year since he'd passed. She had spent so much time worrying about Milo that she hadn't really thought about herself. One thing she was sure of was that, whatever her next move would be, it would include James's memory. It needed to be perfect.

She checked her bank account; she had enough savings that she didn't need to touch the money James had left behind for her and Milo. So, whatever she chose to do, she had enough money to start a new project. Deciding to clear her head, she changed into comfortable jeans and a shirt and grabbed her car keys.

The sun shone beautifully, the perfect weather to have the top down on her car. Milo would still be at school for a few hours, so she needn't worry about him.

Turning up the car stereo, she pulled out of the drive and drove with no real direction in mind. Instead, she let her instincts take the wheel. If her gut said turn left, she would. If it said to turn right, she did. As she drove, she passed a multitude of restaurants, bistros, and cafes.

Proving my point. It's the wrong time and place to be opening a restaurant. There are so many already.

The church at the edge of town had a stream of cars outside. There was a white horse-drawn carriage with two large shire horses with white and pink ribbons laced in their braided manes. Juliette pulled up to the side of the road and watched, with a smile, as a young couple ran to the carriage while family and friends tossed confetti in the air and cheered. Watching with a smile, a voice in her mind said to look left. She turned her head and found an old boarded up storefront for sale. She turned back to watch the newlyweds as their carriage drove past her.

As the blushing bride waved and smiled back at her, a vision hit her like a brick. Ideas flew through her mind at breakneck speed. She was glad she was sitting. She imagined a logo, decorations, marketing. James's face sprang up in her mind's eye.

"It's us," he said.

A stray tear slipped from her eye and rolled down her cheek. *It's us,* she repeated. Pulling out her phone, she called the estate agent's number and arranged a meeting for as soon as possible. Ending the call, she began to make plans in her head. She stepped out of her car, and crossed the street to stand in front of the building. She could see it clear as day.

The name stuck boldly to her mind, and there was no way she would forget it. It was perfect, and with all the designs she had imagined with the name. It was coming out so good in her head that she couldn't wait to make it a reality.

'LOVE & JOY.' The name was simple yet detailed about what she would be giving out to the people. The only thing she had to offer was pure love and joy. Nothing less.

Wedding and event planning. It was everything she could want. She couldn't wait to see women in their gowns and men and women making plans to surprise their significant others. She realized that didn't want to restrict herself just to weddings. There were so many beautiful life events to celebrate. Birthdays, christenings, births, graduations. The list was endless.

She drove home faster than she had intended. She was so excited that she may have run a red light or two. She grabbed paper and pens and began making plans on the kitchen table. She buried herself in drawing designs, listing people to contact, working out prices, and a list of services. She couldn't wait for Milo to come home so she could tell him what she was thinking.

"Wedding and event planning business?" Milo asked, confused. "Wow. I'm surprised. Why that exactly?"

"It's something your father would have loved. And I just can't sit around doing nothing. We both need money, and eventually, I will get tired of sitting around here doing nothing. It's something to give me purpose again. I'm going all in," she told him.

After James died, Milo had assumed the man's responsibility of the house. While it made Juliette proud to see the man he was becoming, he was still a child. In the last year, after school, he had taken to working two jobs to help provide for their needs. Juliette tried to discourage him, but she didn't want to take away his drive or ambition. Also, she was discovering just how much Milo was like his father. Once he set his mind to something, nothing or no one could get him off his task. Besides, she wasn't about to interfere with the process he chose to get through his grief.

"He's a child. You should be doing more. It's not his responsibility," everyone had said. But they had judged her every waking second since James died regardless. *They could judge all they wanted.* She wouldn't let others' opinions shape her life.

"It's fine. Am I going to be part of your team then? I have some really great ideas," Milo said, a thoughtful expression coming over his face.

"Oh, my darling." She hugged her son with so much passion. "You were already part of the team before I thought of what the team would be. I can't wait to hear your ideas."

Milo smiled back at her, realizing how lucky he actually was. From an ever-loving father to a mother who just wanted to see the smile on his face. He felt that the best thing he could do was make her happy by being as happy as he could.

"I'm going to see the agent of the place tomorrow," Juliette said while starting dinner.

After dinner, they sat at the table together in comfortable silence. Milo finished his homework while Juliette doodled more plans. Then, as the day turned to night, Milo headed to his room to relax.

Before bed, Juliette popped her head into his room to check on him and somehow found herself roped into playing a video game she knew nothing about. But, of course, video games had always been Milo and James' thing.

"I'm proud of you, Mom," he told her as they leaned against the headboard of his bed afterwards to sit and talk.

"I'm happy to make you proud." She beamed back and surprised herself by yawning. Without thinking, she placed his duvet over herself before turning the other way and laying her head to sleep.

"Mom. You're getting comfortable. You should go to your room to sleep. I can't carry you, remember?" Milo stuttered.

"I'm sleeping here tonight, though," Juliette said, too tired to do anything but ignore everything her son said right then.

He stopped arguing with her, let out a soft chuckle, and continued to enjoy his game without any disturbance because she was already fast asleep. Milo nodded his head at her with smiles all over his face.

He knew he loved his mother, but right there at that moment, there was something he couldn't ignore. The fact that her love for people was always written all around her, down to her smile, and the way she talked. He hoped the world appreciated her as much as he did.

Milo kissed her gently on the head before switching off his computer and laying down to get some sleep as well. It took a while before he could get to sleep. He stared at his mother, thinking how amazing she was until sleep swept him off his feet.

Two

JULIETTE HAD BEEN the only person interested in the available building, so it was a quick sale. And within two weeks, she had the keys. She never expected things to move so quickly, but she enjoyed the ride and the buzz of excitement.

She quickly arranged for builders to come and help with repairs and electrical issues, and she booked the decorators soon after that. It would take a few weeks, so Juliette advertised the vacancy she needed to fill while waiting. What she needed was an assistant manager, someone to help her with the day-to-day running of *Love & Joy*.

The small town embraced Juliette and her ideas. It may have been a small community, but there was always some celebration happening. And everyone was happy to offload the stress of event planning onto someone else. Before she had even officially opened, she had a string of customers emailing her, asking to book her for their events.

Juliette had her business ready to go at the end of the month. It was perfect. The building wasn't too big or too small. '*Love & Joy Event and Wedding Planning*' sat proudly above the door in big gold letters surrounded by pink and white flowers. Oak flooring, and white walls decorated with art representing different events, were draped with white, pink, and pale blue sheer fabric. There are flowers on every table, and even a vintage tea and coffee station in the back. This was where she had her desk and an area with pink and gold velvet sofas and chairs for consultations. It was perfect. She couldn't wait for her first clients to walk in.

"Wow, Mom, this is....wow," Milo said as he stood in the middle of the room, his eyes darting around to take in what she'd created.

"You like it?"

"I love it....so would Dad," he said with a soft smile.

Her heart fluttered in her chest as she pulled her supportive son in for a hug. James would have indeed loved it. She had one more surprise for Milo, though. Behind her desk was a canvas, hidden by a white tablecloth.

"I have one more thing I would love your opinion on." She grinned.

She walked over and tugged at the cloth, revealing a canvas with the words '*Love & Joy*' written diagonally across it to match the company logo. Above the logo was a picture of Juliette and James on their wedding day and below the logo was a picture of them on the day they brought Milo home from the hospital, wrapped in a pale blue knitted blanket.

"So? What do you think?" she asked excitedly.

"It's.....perfect," he choked, trying to hide his tears.

Juliette ran to her son's side and enveloped him in a hug. This was just as much for him as for her and James's memory.

"I'm so proud to say that you actually own this place now," Milo said again.

Juliette chuckled. "You might have said that already."

"It's because I mean it," Milo insisted.

"Thank you. Now come on, there is still so much work to do," Juliette said, pointing towards the boxes in the corner.

For the rest of the day, Milo and Juliette finished setting up, laying out brochures, price lists, and details of venues. *Love & Joy* wasn't scheduled to open its doors officially for another week, and Juliette still had a small amount of work to do on the website. So, while Juliette worked on the website, Milo took a pile of brochures and business cards and headed out locally, distributing them everywhere he could.

Before they knew it, it was late evening. The streets grew dark, and the rush of cars had slowed. Deciding to stop by a local takeout restaurant on the way home, they packed up and headed out. Back home, tucking into their Chinese, Juliette buzzed with excitement.

Finally, everything was coming together. Her dream was set to become a reality.

"Mom, can I ask you something?" Milo asked before shoving a forkful of noodles into his mouth.

Juliette nodded her response.

"Are you going to be able to run the business on your own?"

"I'm not alone. I have you." She smiled, before hungrily tucking into her duck.

"Mom," Milo replied, giving her a stern look she had only ever seen from James.

"I get that you are worried...."

"Mom, I'm sorry to say, but you haven't been handling stress very well these days. I don't doubt that you can make this business a success. I just don't want you to take on too much," Milo interrupted, his eyes bright with concern.

Juliette let the question linger for a while. She couldn't deny that Milo had a point. She had never coped with stress well, and since she lost her husband, even more so. She knew what Milo said came from a place of love. Finally, after several more mouthfuls of food and a long stare in her direction from Milo, who still was waiting for her answer, Juliette took a slow sip of wine before reaching across to take her son's hand.

"I will be fine, darling. I've advertised for an assistant manager, and I have a few friends who will help me out until I can hire the right staff," she reassured him.

It seemed enough as Milo's shoulders visibly relaxed, and a smile appeared on his face. "Good," he said simply, before turning back toward his food.

The rest of the evening was uneventful. Milo helped clean up after dinner, then he headed upstairs to finish his homework and play video games. Juliette allowed herself time to relax by finishing her wine under a blanket on the couch while watching the latest episodes of Grey's Anatomy. The day's tasks, the food, and wine mixed with the warmth from the fireplace had Juliette's eyes feeling heavy in no time. Yawning, she turned everything off and checked the windows and doors before strolling up to bed.

Upstairs, she lay staring at the ceiling for a while. As soon as her head hit the pillow, her mind raced. Milo's question kept repeating over and over like a warning alarm. She did have friends who could help, but they were not full-time staff and couldn't be there all the time. She knew that she needed to surround herself with the right people, or *Love & Joy* would fail before it even got started. She hoped she hadn't lied to her son. How would she cope with the stress? Eventually, sleep won out, and her mind quietened, allowing her a dreamless sleep.

When she woke the following day, she assumed she had drunk too much wine or slept funny because her body ached in ways she had never felt before. *Milo is right,* she thought, *I haven't been coping well with stress*. But Juliette had a strong mind and told herself she could do this. After a scorching shower that fogged out the bathroom, her aches subsided, leaving her muscles feeling like butter. She heard Milo wake shortly after her. He gave her a brief smile as they passed each other on the landing while he headed to the family bathroom to prepare for school. Juliette fixed up some fresh orange juice, coffee, and chocolate chip pancakes and set them out on the table, waiting for Milo.

Loading up her to-do list on her phone, she typed in a few more entries, ensuring that everything was in full order. To Juliette, to-do lists were her way of eliminating stress. She liked to know what needed to be done and when. She felt a sense of gratification and satisfaction when she got to click the completed tab next to each task. With each tick off her list, she felt her stresses vanish. She had the perfect plan in mind and was ready to get down to work.

Milo and Juliette finished breakfast before Milo ran to catch the school bus. Finally, alone Juliette fired off a round of texts, confirming who was due to meet her at *Love & Joy,* and telling them that she would be roughly half an hour.

She arrived at *Love & Joy* ten minutes before her friends were due to arrive. Her skin prickled with goosebumps, and every hair on her body stood on end as she looked up at the sign. It was everything she had hoped for. She couldn't wait to bring so much love and joy into people's events, to be a part of their happy memories like James had been for her.

Heading inside, a wall of fragrance hit her from all the fresh flowers in the room. If happiness had a scent, this was it. She flung open the curtains and turned on the stereo playing soft acoustic covers of some of her favourite songs, mixed with a few classical instrumental covers. Light engulfed the space highlighting all the soft colours of the furniture, artwork, and decorations. It was as though she were seeing the place through fresh eyes for the first time. She never wanted that feeling of awe to end.

She headed to the coffee station and brewed a fresh pot, at the same time, boiling the kettle for her friends who preferred tea. And she sat at her desk patiently waiting for them to arrive, she soaked up all the feelings of happiness that her new life gave to her. Gratitude filled her as she thought about her friends. While some didn't get her reasoning, they still cheered her on and were there to help.

She heard the engines purr to a stop outside, and the soft giggles of her friends as they pulled into the small car park out front. The small bell above the door indicated their arrival, and she beamed as they stood frozen in the doorway. Eyes scanned every corner, and smiles beamed back at her before a chorus of excited screams filled the room.

"Oh my God, Juliette. This place is so beautiful!" Rebecca cheered as she danced excitedly over to Juliette.

"You are so talented," chirped Christine.

"I never knew you had it in you. You go girly!" Lauren piped up, adding her excitement to that of the others.

Juliette hugged her friends in turn. Her cheeks hurt from smiling so widely. Her eyes flashed with tears of joy from her friends' outpouring of love and admiration.

"Thanks, girls, it means a lot. And thank you all so much for helping me out," she said as she poured everyone a drink.

"We are happy to help. I just wish I could do more. With work and the kids, it's hard to have any kind of life lately," Lauren said, settling into the plush pink couch next to the tea and coffee station.

"Don't apologize. I appreciate everything you guys do for me.

Besides, I will be fine once I hire someone permanently," Juliette answered.

"How's that going, by the way?" Christine asked while she perused the artwork on the walls.

"I've got a few interviews lined up today, actually. So, it's the first thing on the to-do list."

"Ok, so let's get started. What are our jobs?" beamed Rebecca.

They had a quick catch-up and some girl chat while they finished their drinks. After that, Juliette gave each of her friends a task for the day, and they compared schedules to make sure Juliette always had a helping hand. Rebecca could help on Monday and Wednesdays, Christine on Tuesdays and Fridays, and Lauren made herself free on weekends. Once the scheduling was out of the way, each went about their tasks. Lauren organized the diary and called the list of potential clients to set up appointments. Christine arranged meetings with vendors to secure a working relationship, and Rebecca was set to help with interviews. Rebecca worked in recruitment, so it made sense for her to help vet the prospective candidates.

Christine and Lauren had a very productive and successful day, but Rebecca and Juliette began to worry as they conducted interview after interview. No one seemed to be the right fit. The first candidate was too young, and the next didn't have enough experience. One girl sat and looked disapprovingly down her nose at everyone and the decor, and another made it clear that she didn't really want to be there. Juliette began to feel her shoulders tense and her neck ache.

Whenever she was stressed, she carried it in her bones and joints. Milo's concerns circled her head. She truly wasn't dealing with stress well lately.

"This is hopeless," she complained after the latest candidate had left. "What am I going to do?" she asked Rebecca as she rubbed the back of her neck, trying to release the tension.

"Relax, we still have one more interview to go, and if it sucks, well, I'm sure I can pull a few strings at work and help you find someone." Rebecca smiled, as she handed Juliette yet another coffee. Juliette had lost track of how many she'd had, but if her shaking hands were any indication, it had to be one cup too many.

Busying themselves with other tasks, neither Rebecca nor Juliette realized the time had passed by until the bell rang, and a tall, dark, handsome man walked in with his suit jacket draped over his arm. He wore a single diamond stud in his left ear. His dark three-piece suit had to be designer, from its clean-cut lines and expensive-looking fabric. His hair was cut short, and Juliette wondered if he wore eyeliner from how much his deep brown eyes stood out.

"Hello, I'm here to interview for the assistant manager position," he smiled, walking over with the stride of a supermodel, holding out his hand to Rebecca and Juliette with confidence and panache.

Juliette smiled as he shook her hand. She always thought you could tell a lot about a person from their handshake, which gave her a good feeling.

"Hi, I'm Juliette, owner of *Love & Joy*. This is my friend Rebecca, and you are?"

"Dante Jones," he replied.

"Come take a seat. Would you like a drink?" Rebecca asked.

"Oh yes, please."

"Tea or coffee?" Juliette asked.

"Do you have Earl Grey? With a squeeze of lemon and a dash of honey?" Dante asked, draping his jacket off the back of the chair in front of Juliette's desk.

He sat back and crossed one leg over the other, his eyes locked on the picture behind the desk. "That picture is stunning," Dante said.

Juliette smiled and handed him his tea. She was becoming tearful at the idea of explaining to someone new that James was no longer there. She tried several times to speak, smiling back each time she failed. Dante leaned forward and rested his hand over hers.

"Oh sweetie, don't worry. I don't need to know. But I will say, your love for him shines brightly in your eyes. He must have been something special," Dante said softly, stroking his thumb gently over her hand before sitting back, instantly resuming his professional demeanour.

The interview was a huge success. Dante had experience in event planning and customer service. He was charismatic and charming, and soon after, Lauren and Christine joined the conversation. Everyone loved him and agreed he was perfect for the job. They offered him the position on the spot.

⌀

Love & Joy opened soon after, and Juliette was surprised by how much of a success it had turned out to be. They had to start a waiting list she had so many inquiries. Dante had proven to be a huge help. After several months, he and Juliette had become close friends. She found the fifteen-year age gap was precisely what she needed in a friend. He offered her advice and guidance she couldn't get from her other friends. And after he grew comfortable around her, he confided in her that he was gay. Juliette had thought he felt forced to tell her because of Laurens's constant flirting, but he assured her it was not that. Having a strong gay man on the team opened a whole new revenue of clientele. He helped arrange events for local drag queens, same-sex couples, and even a few LGBTQ+ meetings, and support rallies.

With Dante's and Milo's help and constant support, Rebecca, Lauren, and Christine slowly took their leave and allowed Juliette to run her business her own way. Occasionally, they would pop in and lend a hand, but they knew Juliette had things covered.

"Hey sweetie, what seems to be troubling you?" Dante asked, handing Juliette a fresh cup of tea.

It had been a long day, and now *Love & Joy* had closed its door for the night. Juliette finally had a moment to relax. Over the last few months, she had been so busy that *Love & Joy* had taken up a large chunk of her time. While Milo helped out whenever he could, guilt tugged at her stomach. She worried that she had been neglecting her son.

"I'm fine." She smiled back, but her heart was not in it.

Dance sat in front of her desk and leaned back, crossing one leg over the other. He cocked a perfectly groomed eyebrow and gave Juliette a look that she had become used to seeing, which meant he knew she was lying. Whenever Dante gave her that look, she knew she couldn't keep quiet. He had become a good friend and confidante and had a fantastic ability to read people, Juliette included.

"Talk to me, sweetie," he said, his voice was kind.

Juliette sighed deeply. "I'm worried I have let *Love & Joy* take over my life, and I have been neglecting my son. I promised James before he died that I would be the best mother I could be, and I feel like I'm letting him down."

"Hasn't he just given up one of his jobs? Taken more time to focus on his own interests?"

"Yes."

"...and why do you think that is?" Dante asked, sipping his cappuccino.

Juliette couldn't answer. She knew Dante had a point but couldn't figure out what it was. It was clear he was allowing her a few moments to try and figure it out on her own before he continued.

"Sweetie, when I started here, that boy worked two jobs after school and was helping out here. He wanted to take care of you. But now that you have succeeded in this place, he allowed himself to give up on that role. He believes in you. You are not letting him down at all. Besides, I have watched Milo. He may be young, but he is a competent young man. You raised him well. Trust him," Dante reassured her.

She smiled. "You always know just what to say."

"It's one of my many gifts. If it still worries you, try talking to him. I'm sure he will tell you the same."

With Dante's reassuring words and a fresh perspective, Juliette wished Dante goodnight and headed home. When she arrived, she found Milo watching a movie on the sofa with his friend Pete.

"Hey, Mom, dinner is in the oven. I've taken care of all the chores, and I've posted the checks for this month's bills," Milo said as she came in, a proud smile on his face.

"What? You didn't have to do all that," she protested, feeling now more than ever that she was letting him down.

He frowned, not expecting this response. "It's cool. I like doing it."

"Can I have a word?" Juliette asked, waving hello to Pete and heading into the kitchen to pour a cold glass of wine.

"What's up?" Milo asked, grabbing two sodas from the fridge.

Juliette voiced her concerns and, with each word, felt the tension she had been carrying around in her shoulders melt away. She needed Milo to know how important he was to her and that no matter how responsible he was, she was still his mother and wanted him to enjoy life as a kid for as long as possible.

Milo walked around the kitchen island and wrapped his mother in a hug, cupping her face, and forcing her to look at him.

"Mom, I appreciate everything you do for me. I don't do these things because I have to. I do them because we're family. You and Dad raised me well. I'm more than capable of looking after myself. I also know you will be there if I need you. I love you, Mom, and I always will." Milo smiled.

Juliette felt her heart swell with pride. This young man was her son. *He may be young, but he was a man in every sense of the word.*

"I'm so proud of you," she said, choking up a little as she tried to force the words past the lump in her throat. She pulled him in for a tighter hug before letting him head back to his friend. "We raised him well," she said, raising her glass in a silent toast to the picture of James she kept on the shelf above the kitchen counter.

Three

BIRTHDAYS, Weddings, Bar Mitzvahs, Anniversaries, Corporate Events. The list grew on and on. With each passing event, Juliette hadn't noticed the year go by. Dante, Rebecca, Milo, Christine, and Lauren organized an intimate surprise celebration for Juliette to congratulate her on *Love & Joy's* first birthday and a year of success.

"I'm so lucky to have such a great group of people around me. Thank you so much, guys. I couldn't have done this without you," Juliette choked up a little as she raised a toast to her friends.

"Oh please, we hardly helped at all. This is all you....well, you and Dante. Enjoy it," Lauren cheered.

"There is something I have been meaning to ask you. I hope you don't think I'm overstepping the mark," Dante whispered, pulling Juliette aside from the group as the others chatted, danced, and enjoyed champagne and drifted around the store.

"Sure, what's up?"

Dante went to his desk and pulled out a small red folder, handing it to Juliette. He waited for her response. He had been working on the presentation for a few weeks. And if she agreed, he had the next steps all planned out.

"What this? A business proposal?" she asked, skimming over the pages.

"Expansion, actually. The unit next door is about to go on the market. With all the business we have, I think we could expand into next door, maybe even hire another member for the team," Dante ventured.

"Are you sure we can do it?"

Dante smiled and talked Juliette through his proposal. He explained all the extra business they could take in, outlined a five-year growth plan, and extrapolated potential earnings using the profits they had already made as a basis. He wanted to hear her opinion before telling her he had already scheduled an appointment with the estate agent for the following week.

"I love it. Let's do it!" Juliette beamed as she looked through the documents a second time, with a new appreciation for all the work he'd done in putting this proposal together.

"Really?"

"Of course, let's celebrate....Guys, Dante and I have some news," Juliette cheered, taking Dante by the hand and rejoining the group.

Dante took care of everything to do with purchasing the unit next door. He arranged for the builders to come and knock a wall through to join the two properties. Juliette worked from home to avoid interrupting business while the renovation was underway. Dante jumped back into action with decorating while Rebecca helped with the interview process when it was clear to move back in.

Love & Joy had gained an impressive reputation. As soon as word got out that there was a job opening, Juliette was inundated with applications. Vetting the candidates the second time around proved trickier than the first. This time around, however, everyone seemed perfect for the job and had come super prepared.

"How am I going to choose?" Juliette groaned as she sat down for lunch with her friends.

"We will get there, sweetie, don't you worry." Dante smiled, greeting

Rebecca with a kiss on each cheek. "How many more do you have to interview?"

"Thankfully, there is only one person left," Rebecca answered.

"Mind if I sit in?" Dante asked, eager to do his part to help out.

"Please do. We can use all the help we can get," Rebecca sighed, the day's efforts clearly putting a strain on her.

"You make this job easier for me. I'm so glad I picked you for this role. I truly value your input. I wouldn't be expanding if it wasn't for you," Juliette never failed to remind Dante of how amazing he was and how happy she was to have him on her side.

"Stop it, or my head will grow so big I won't be able to get it out the door," Dante joked, making everyone erupt into laughter.

They all were chatting and gossiping over lunch when the doorbell rang. A tall slim, dark-haired beauty walked in with her baby strapped to her chest.

"Hi, how can we help you? Are you hoping to plan an event for this little darling?" Dante greeted the woman shaking her hand and leading her to the consultation area.

"No, actually, I'm here for my interview. I'm Avery Lannister." The woman smiled weakly, looking nervous and awkward. "I'm so sorry, my babysitter cancelled last minute, and I didn't want to miss out on such a wonderful opportunity."

"No problem at all. Would you like a drink?" Juliette beamed, joining Dante and Avery at the table.

"No, thank you." Avery smiled, relaxing a little.

"So, tell us about yourself," Dante began, taking out his notebook and pen and scanning over Avery's resume.

"Um.... My name is Avery, and this is my beautiful daughter Emma. I'm a recently single mother. Emma is adopted, and.....To be candid, while I don't have a lot of experience with event planning, I'm a goal-orientated person and eager to learn. I have proven success in sales and customer service, and I'm looking for a job that will allow me the freedom to continue having a hand in raising my daughter. I don't want her raised by a nanny," Avery said.

Dante and Juliette sat stunned. It was refreshing to have someone speak so clearly and honestly about what they wanted. The others they had interviewed, while all very good, never seemed genuine. While experience was important, for Juliette, finding someone who would gel well with the team was just as important.

After the standard interview questions were out the way, Dante excused himself to call up a few of Avery's references while Juliette continued to chat with her. Avery was visibly nervous at first.

Understandably so, as not many employers would welcome a prospective candidate turning up with a baby strapped to their chest. However, when Juliette explained why she opened *Love & Joy* and how her son helped out every once in a while, Avery opened up and told her story.

"Being transgender, it was so hard for me and my ex to find an adoption agency who would work with us. After my transition, I still felt like something was missing. When Emma came along, I felt complete. Only, once the novelty of having a baby wore off and the responsibility kicked in, Gemma, my girlfriend, left. I don't mind raising Emma alone, but I don't want to be missing out on the big milestones, you know?" Avery said.

"I hear you. And thank you for sharing your story. So, is Avery your legal name...did you...?" Juliette knew what she wanted to ask, but as an aspiring ally, it was sometimes tricky to know what was and wasn't okay to ask or even how to ask certain questions. She didn't want to offend Avery and felt honoured that she had chosen to open up so freely. At the same time, you needed to know what name to put on the documentation when hiring someone.

Avery chuckled. "It's okay to ask. Avery is actually my birth name. It's like my parents knew I'd need a gender-neutral name later in life."

"That's beautiful. I love that." Juliette smiled.

She couldn't quite explain it, but she felt a connection, a sort of bond with Avery. Her gut told her that she was the person to hire. She couldn't wait for Dante to get back to tell him all about her. Finally, Dante rejoined them with a beaming smile on his face.

"Well, your references couldn't speak highly enough of you. You made quite the impression."

"Well, I feel like that's all we need. Dante. What do you think?" Juliette asked.

Juliette and Dante had grown so close that he knew what she was asking with the look in her eyes and the tilt of her head. He winked back at her, and they turned to Avery with a smile.

"Welcome to *Love & Joy*," they cheered in unison.

❦

Dante and Juliette told Avery she could start the following Monday. Still, Avery was so happy someone had given her a chance after being discriminated against so many times before that she insisted she begin immediately. It was agreed that Avery could bring Emma to work with her, which made Avery even happier.

She turned out to be the perfect fit for the team. Everyone loved her, and the team accepted her in no time at all. Milo was happy to help with Emma without being asked most of the time. It warmed Juliette's heart seeing a softer, less serious side of her son.

They split their duties equally. Avery took care of new clients and set up the new extended part of the store, while Dante took over corporate events, and Juliette jumped into taking over weddings. Juliette loved every part of *Love & Joy*, but she had a soft spot for helping plan weddings. They had been her main goal when she started the business.

The clients loved the family feel of the store. Emma had unintentionally become a just as vital part of the team. Juliette added Avery to the store website, and as the customers became more familiar with her, she brought in new clientele. It seemed the business was expanding every day in ways Juliette had never expected. Soon they were getting bookings from couples and families from out of town.

Avery joked a few times that the business could afford to franchise and venture into other cities and maybe even the big cities by another year two. Juliette loved that her new friends had such passion for the business and faith in her, but the idea of the business growing so quickly scared her a little. In the future, yes, it would be a great plan, but right now, Juliette was happy in her small-town bubble with her friends turned family.

With the business running a lot smoother now with an extra set of hands on board, Juliette found she had a little more time to herself. This coincided with a deep-seated need she hadn't been able to talk to anybody about just yet. She'd been keeping a secret for the past year and a half that she found difficult to share.

While she was happy with her business and loved her new life, she had let herself slide in the process of looking after everyone else. Before she opened her business, she had bumped into an old college friend who had made a snippy comment about her weight. Juliette couldn't deny that she had put on a few pounds.

With the business keeping her so busy, she'd been ignoring her old exercise routines and making food choices that were quick and easy, and tended to be not as nutritious as she might have liked. She was actually the heaviest she had ever been. And while she had never been one to worry too much about her weight, that was probably because it had never been an issue.

Until now.

Lately, she'd been less than satisfied with her appearance. Many a night, she would go to her room and stare at herself in the mirror, picking herself apart and hating what she saw. Then the morning would come around, and she would be too busy to think about it again until she was alone with her own thoughts. Finally, with Dante and Avery both managing the business so well, she decided it was time to work on herself.

She started by creating a new schedule. For two days a week, Avery and Dante would take care of everything without her. Juliette could then take these days off and head to the gym. She found the break away from everything was just what she needed and working out had become a new form of therapy for her. Be it a few pool lengths, aerobics class, or weight training, slowly, as she saw her body changing, her confidence returned.

This solved one of her problems. The other though was not quite so simple.

Her heart still belonged to James. And while she never considered herself lonely, she did notice her heart ached a little with each new wedding she helped to plan. Seeing so much love on a day-to-day basis made her long for James. It may have been almost two and a half years since he passed, but suddenly she found her wounds regarding his loss hadn't completely healed. Every once in a while, she would cry herself to sleep clutching one of his shirts. She wished he could see what she was doing now. She even felt guilty that it had taken losing him for her to venture out into business. She dreamt of what it would be like if James was still there, involved in *Love & Joy*. He would have been such a great partner in the enterprise.

Baby, I miss you.

"Mom, can I talk to you?" Milo asked one morning when she woke up groggy after crying herself to sleep again. It was happening more often these days.

When Juliette joined him in the kitchen, she found he had already made a beautiful breakfast of chocolate chip pancakes, bacon, and eggs.

"Sure," she replied, one eyebrow raising at the sight of so much food.

"I noticed how Avery and Dante are excited about the speed dating event coming up. The first event of its kind for *Love & Joy*. I also noticed how you are not involved in the event. Are you okay? I have heard you crying yourself to sleep a few times." He paused, shifting uncomfortably before finally asking, "Are you lonely?"

Milo's question stunned Juliette. She honestly didn't know how to answer. Was she okay? Was she lonely? Did she want to start dating again? Guilt twisted her stomach at the thought of replacing James, but a voice in the back of her mind told her it was okay to want to move forward.

When she didn't answer, Milo continued, "Dad would want you to be happy. You know that, right? If you wanted to start dating again, I'd be cool with it."

"Honey..."

"No, Mom, just think about it, ok? And you know, I'm always here if you want to talk," he kissed her on the cheek and headed off to school.

Alone in the kitchen, Juliette tucked into the food Milo had prepared, while thinking long and hard about what her son had said. He would be a senior soon, and he'd be thinking of new adventures.

How did he become so insightful? She never wanted to stop loving James. More importantly, she didn't have time for dating. It had been so long since she had last been on a date, the thought of meeting someone new was scary. Of course, she missed being loved by someone. The cozy nights in, romantic gestures, and the rush of new love. *Maybe he is right. Perhaps I should join the event,* she finally thought.

Dante and Avery were thrilled when Juliette told them she would like to be involved. She opened up to them about how she'd been feeling and the awkward conversation she had with her son.

"You don't need to rush into anything. Why not sign up for the event? You never know. It might help you decide what you really want," Avery said as she rocked Emma back to sleep.

Juliette felt the beginnings of a smile, the first she'd genuinely wanted to smile in a long time. "You're right. I love you guys."

"We love you too, sweetie. But, if you are going speed dating, I'm giving you a make-over. Not that you need it, but let's get you looking fabulous," Dante said, already dialling his favourite stylist.

Before she knew it, the speed dating event was upon them. Dante and Avery had signed up, too, in a show of support. Milo happily volunteered to take care of Emma. Juliette went in with an open mind, telling herself she was just there to have fun and see what happened.

As it turned out, Juliette did have a lot of fun at the event but didn't feel the spark her heart craved with anyone. One thing she did find was her new awareness. She was ready to find someone to love. She decided she was open to new love but would relax and let love find her.

Dante, on the other hand, managed to grab a date with a dentist named Dave, who he talked about constantly for the following month. Avery was very picky about who she chose to date. Emma was her first priority. She conceded to a date with Steve the barista at the coffee shop down the street after he made her laugh till her sides hurt. They weren't a good fit, but he later introduced her to Emily, who turned out to be a little too intense for Avery. Eventually, Avery admitted she wasn't ready for anything serious but was happy to date, just for fun.

"I have all I need with my daughter. She is the love of my life," she said, and shrugged.

"You are so beautiful, Avery," Juliette told her. "I'll let love find me, and I know when you are ready, love will find you too."

Four

"WHAT ARE YOU DOING HERE? Your next appointment isn't until two this afternoon. We've got this. Go relax," Dante ordered the moment Juliette strode in.

"I thought I had an appointment with the Carmers at ten?"

"They came in early. I've already dealt with them," Avery informed her.

"Oh...thank you." Juliette smiled.

Juliette felt terrible for rushing from home down to the office without even fixing something for Milo to eat before going to school. He had told her that it was okay, but she still felt terrible about it.

"Stop it! I know that look. Milo is fine," Dante said, wagging his finger at Juliette.

Avery laughed. "It still amazes me how you can read everyone like that. Are you sure you are not psychic?"

Dante shrugged and winked at Juliette.

"Sorry, old habits die hard," she smiled, "I don't know what to do with myself now," she said, twiddling her thumbs.

"Get your nails done. Pamper yourself. You deserve it." Dante pointed toward the door, laughing. "Go already!"

"You know what? I think I will," Juliette said.

Juliette managed to get a last-minute appointment with Clips and Claws boutique around the corner and settled into having herself pampered. Then, with a glass of champagne in hand, she closed her eyes and let the manicurist work her magic. Finally, she decided on a new haircut, nothing too drastic, just a short, graduated bob. Of course, some highlights were in order, so she requested that as well, ending with a French manicure to match her toes.

Hours later, Dante and Avery wolf-whistled upon her arrival back to the office. Juliette felt better than she had in ages. She settled into her desk and prepared a few extra touches for her presentation for her late afternoon appointment. Avery informed her that Juliette was due to be meeting a single dad setting up a birthday party for his young daughter.

Juliette brought up princess party pictures from past events, animal kingdoms, and a host of other themed children's events. She prepared her list of vendors and her questionnaire.

Later that afternoon, Juliette was seated in her office, ready for the meeting, when a man walked in with a young girl bouncing by his side.

The girl looked so happy, and one could easily tell that she deeply loved her dad. A true daddy's girl. She looked up at her father like he was a celebrity and beamed with pride with every step. It was evident by the way he doted on her that he adored her in return. The expensive doll in her arms, and the quality of clothing the little girl wore gave hints that his daughter had the best of everything. He maybe even spoiled her a little.

Juliette was rendered speechless. Her new client was handsome, charismatic, and well built. Easily six foot five, or maybe taller, he was clearly a man who took pride in his appearance. He introduced himself and his daughter. Even the way he spoke was sexy.

Juliette needed to pull herself together instead of standing there staring, dumbfounded. Shaking her head to bring herself out of her stupor, she forced a smile and gestured for them to take a seat.

Get a hold of yourself, Julie,

Juliette shuffled the papers on her desk, forcing herself to snap back into professional mode by reminding her that this man was here for a reason, and it was up to her to make sure his event went off without a hitch.

"So, Mr. Field..."

"Damian," he interrupted.

"Excuse me?"

He smiled. "Please, call me Damian."

Juliette felt herself blush as she continued with her presentation. The meeting only took about thirty minutes for them to conclude. Damian loved everything about the samples that Juliette showed him. But, since his daughter didn't show too much interest in any particular one, Damian told her to do something different for them. Something unique, that his daughter would really like.

By now, Juliette was used to talking to children about what they wanted their birthday party to be like. Patiently, she asked Cara several questions about what she wanted to do. She also spent some time getting to know Cara's favourite Disney princess, tv shows, and anything else she could to determine what the little girl would like. Thankfully, this questioning revealed nothing too difficult. She scribbled down a few ideas, already looking forward to being able to be a little more creative than usual with this particular party.

"I shall have a new presentation worked up for you by this time tomorrow for you to review," she informed Cara solemnly.

The little girl seemed to relish being treated like an adult. It was plain to see that she relished the idea of making all the decisions. She was adorable. Damian and Juliette exchanged numbers so that they could finalize the financial details such as the budget and payment information. From the initial discussion, Juliette got the feeling that the budget would be quite generous for Cara's birthday party. By extension, so would her fee. If she was right, this party might take their business to a different level altogether.

He thanked her and everyone else in the office before heading out.

A gentleman. All that and he's a gentleman too.

Juliette was definitely smitten.

Damian returned the next day with Cara. After her new presentation, Cara cheered with excitement. The date was set for three weeks from now.

Cara was a unique little girl. She loved a cartoon series called Pirate Warriors but was also feminine and loved princesses and animals. So, the theme she settled on for her party was Pirate Princess Warriors.

To Juliette's delight it was just as she'd thought. The sky was definitely the limit where the budget was concerned.

Juliette spent the following weeks arranging for a pirate ship experience on the local lake. After tea on the deck, there would be princess makeovers and an instructor to show the children how to fight like pirates – with Styrofoam swords, of course. After that, she arranged for a cake and party back on dry land, ending with pony rides and a petting zoo. It was a lot to cram into one party, but Juliette lived for the chaos.

"Are you texting him again?" Avery asked in hushed tones.

"I'm just making sure he is happy with the plans," Juliette answered, only just keeping herself from doing something absolutely childish and sticking her tongue out at her employee.

"I think someone has a crush," Dante teased.

Juliette tried to deny it, but somehow Damien occupied her thoughts a lot lately. She couldn't seem to get him out of her mind no matter how much she tried – and it wasn't the upcoming party she was thinking about. She couldn't pinpoint what it was about him. She was drawn to him like a moth to a flame, smiling and blushing every time he replied to her texts.

She told Dante and Avery that it was all business between them. But truth be told, she and Damien had been exchanging many messages that were not so business-related. She wasn't the only one feeling this way either. They talked about going on an official date once the party was over. What was even more romantic was how she woke up every morning to a text saying, *'Good morning, beautiful.'* She felt a spark of chemistry between herself and Damian and couldn't wait for Cara's birthday so she could officially see him again.

The birthday party came quickly and was executed perfectly, just like she had planned. Cara hugged her and thanked her repeatedly for the best party ever. Dante and Avery spent the day commenting on how they had noticed the spark between Juliette and Damian and encouraged her to go for it.

"Thank you for making Cara's birthday so special. You and your team are amazing....but you, especially," Damian thanked her, kissing her on the cheek, and sending a shiver down her spine.

"It was my pleasure."

"Then allow me to have the pleasure of a date, so I can thank you properly."

"She would love to. I'll text you her calendar," Dante butted in, making both Damian and Juliette laugh.

◦ ℓ

Their first date was a simple meal at *Italia Roma*. The two of them connected so well that it was as if they had known each other for years. They had a lot in common, and Damian was charming, sensitive, and attentive. The months that followed found them keeping each other up late nights talking on the phone. Damian and Juliette decided to keep things quiet until they made things official. Still, once the gifts started arriving at the office, Dante and Avery began asking questions, even though it was apparent they knew who they were from. First, there were flowers with love notes that were penned from the heart. Sweet poems and words of encouragement became almost daily occurrences.

"So, are you official?" Avery poked at Juliette as she arranged beautiful bouquet of lilies in a crystal vase.

"We aren't anything yet. I'm in no rush. Neither is he."

"He seems smitten to me," Dante agreed.

Juliette thought over what she had learned about Damian. Damian was two years older than Juliette. His ex-fiancé had left him immediately after his daughter was born. She returned sometime the previous year, promising to be a better person who wanted to be there for her daughter and him. Domain wished to think the best of her and do what was right for his daughter, but it turned out that his trust was misplaced because she left them weeks later. She had only come back for money.

Afterwards, he vowed to never have anything to do with her again, no matter how much she begged. With all that, she couldn't blame him for guarding his, and his daughter's, hearts and wanting to take things slow. Juliette understood. Truth be told, she still held a flame for James and didn't want to lose that.

After another month, Juliette decided to confide in Milo about her new relationship. While they still hadn't made things official, she thought he had a right to know. He may have encouraged her to date, but she still felt guilty about moving on. And if Milo wasn't okay with it, she planned to call it all off.

"Mom, are you happy?" he asked when she told him what had been going on.

"Yes."

"Then so am I."

Juliette beamed. "What did I do to deserve a son like you?" she asked, giving Milo a fierce hug.

Her phone buzzed several times in her pocket, interrupting their mother/son moment. It was Dante.

"Sweetie, you need to get back here right away. There is someone here. She won't tell me her name, but she is *pissed*. She is demanding to speak with you." Dante sounded panicked, and Juliette could hear Avery in the background trying to calm the woman down, as her screaming made Emma, now a toddler, start to cry.

"I will be right there!" She put the phone down and grabbed her keys, "Sorry honey, there is a pickle at the office, have a good day at school," she kissed Milo and ran out the door.

When she walked into *Love & Joy*, the bell above the door alerted everyone of Juliette's arrival.

A tall blonde woman with a face like thunder was screaming at Dante and Avery. Dante was holding his phone as though contemplating calling the police.

"Excuse me, but I would appreciate it if you didn't speak to my team like that," Juliette said as politely as she could as she rushed to her team's defence. She put a hand up to stall Dante until she could get a read on the situation.

The angry woman spun around, a look of hatred as hot as fire burned in her eyes, freezing Juliette in place.

"Are you Juliette?" she screamed.

"Yes, and you...."

But unfortunately, Juliette didn't get a chance to finish her sentence before the woman swung, slapping Juliette across the cheek. An angry red handprint instantly appeared across Juliette's stunned face.

"Back off!" the woman spat, silencing the room.

"Excuse...me?" Juliette stuttered, stunned, speechless, holding her hand to her throbbing cheek. She could hear Dante dialling in the background.

Five

"WHO ARE YOU?" Juliette finally managed to ask.

The woman laughed like a psychopath with maddened, crazed eyes darting around the room. As if it was an insult to her that no one knew who she was. "You know damn right who I am. Don't play like you don't," the woman screamed.

"I'm sorry." Juliette said, "but can you please tell me what is going on exactly?"

The woman laughed hard again and stared at her for a few seconds before whirling and stalking around the room, pacing like a caged animal, her eyes never leaving Juliette.

"Homewrecker! Stay away from my man! Or next time, I won't play so nice," she snarled.

"Your man? Are you Damian's ex-fiancé?" Juliette looked at Dante who had paused with his finger over the button which would connect his call. He had the same confused expression since the whole thing started.

Juliette felt her heart break a little, and even though she actually trusted Damian, she had a feeling that the woman could be telling the truth. No one could go that crazy over a relationship that didn't exist. Juliette had built a business on spreading Love, Joy, and Happiness.

This was the furthest thing from what she wanted. She never wanted to break up a family. She'd thought she knew so much about Damian. But as this woman screamed at her, Juliette questioned whether she really knew him at all.

"I'm so sorry. He told me you had broken up. I never would have gone near him if I had known," Juliette said, her hands up in a placating gesture as she pleaded with the woman to understand.

"I know him more than you do, and he is a man of many women. Never satisfied by just one. You are one of a long queue, you are nothing special, believe me. I stay with him despite my broken heart, for the love of our daughter. If you don't believe me, ask him about Nia. Watch his jaw drop," the woman said before storming out.

Juliette reached for a chair, her head spinning with all this new information. Dante pocketed his phone as he and Avery rushed to her side, helping her to her seat. Within moments, the doorbell rang again. This time Damian walked through the door.

"He has got some nerve. Do you think he bumped into her as she left?" Avery snarled when she saw who it was.

"Juliette? What's wrong?" Damian panicked, rushing over to her.

Dante was quicker though and stepped between them. "I don't think so. You stay away from her."

"Dante, it's fine. Can you two leave us for a moment?" Juliette barely got out the words, so shaken was she by the encounter.

Reluctantly, Dante and Avery headed to the next room, but Juliette knew they had their ears pressed against the door. If she needed them, they'd be there in an instant.

She stood eye to eye with Damian, her eyes filled with tears. She had told Damian all about James, not just about the heartbreak from losing her love, but about the betrayal of trust she felt in thinking he had known he'd been sick. And here all Damian had done was lie to her.

"Who's Nia?" Juliette went straight to the point.

Damian's jaw dropped for the briefest of moments before he recovered himself with a rough clearing of his throat. "She's an ex. You know that. She's the one I told you about. She's Cara's mother," Damian explained patiently.

"I would have believed you if she had not been here moments

before, screaming that she is still your fiancé. I would have believed you if she hadn't slapped my face for going near you. A woman doesn't get that angry about an ex." Juliette pointed to the red handprint still across her face that had begun to swell.

"Nia was here?" Damian asked, clearly taken aback by the injury now that he noticed it. "What was she doing here?"

"You tell me!" Juliette yelled at him.

Damian stood silent, just as surprised by Juliette's outburst as she was.

"I'm so sorry she came here. I don't know how she found out about us. I didn't even know she was back in town."

"Just go, Damian. I don't think there is anything you can say right now that will make any of this go away. I have built my business on bringing people together. If word got out that I had broken up an *engagement*? My business would be ruined!" Juliette spoke.

"You didn't break us up. We are not together. She left. I don't want her, Juliette. I want *you*. I love *you*," Damian said, his eyes growing wide as the words left his lips.

It was the first time he had said it. Juliette expected to feel overjoyed. But Nia's appearance overshadowed the moment leaving Damian's words hollow against Juliette's ears.

"Just go." Juliette turned away, not wanting him to see her tears.

"Tell me you don't feel the same. Tell me you feel nothing, and I will go and never bother you again."

Juliette couldn't answer. She couldn't say whether it was love or infatuation, but she definitely felt something for him. *Maybe it is love. Only love can hurt this bad.*

"Juliette. Do you *really* think I would introduce you to my daughter if I was still with her mother?" Damian pleaded.

Still, Juliette said nothing. She wanted to believe him, but she needed to think things over with a clear mind first.

"Look, I'm going to go. But promise me you will think things through and call me when you are ready. I don't want to rush you, but I don't want us to give up on something before we even have a chance." Damien placed a hand on Juliette's shoulder, slowly turning her to face him. "Please, promise me?"

"I'll think about it," she finally agreed.

Six

JULIETTE DIDN'T KNOW what to believe. A part of her wanted so badly to believe Damian. Indeed, if he was still with Nia, he wouldn't have let Cara be around while they were together, out of fear she'd reveal his secrets. It is so easy for someone so young to be completely innocent and honest. What did Nia mean about a string of women? Now that Damian had left, Juliette's mind swam with questions.

"Hey sweetie, are you ok?" Dante asked, approaching Juliette with the same caution one might approach a rabid dog.

"Not really," Juliette croaked, finally allowing her tears to fall.

Avery and Dante rushed over, wrapping themselves around her in a group hug. Avery sat Juliette down while Dante closed the shop. Their next appointment wasn't scheduled until late afternoon, so they could afford to take a few hours to themselves. Offering words of wisdom and a fresh set of eyes, they talked things through. The possibility of Nia lying; the chance that Damian could be telling the truth. Both Dante and Avery agreed that Juliette needed to sit down and talk with him. Even if it was to call it quits, she at least needed to know where she stood.

"Oh sweetie, you are in love with him, aren't you?" Dante asked.

"I don't know."

"Yes, you do. You are just too scared to admit it," Avery said, giving Juliette's hand a comforting squeeze.

"You are right. I do love him. But how? It's so soon. There is still so much we don't know about each other, and now this." Juliette admitted.

"Love can't be explained; it's a magical thing like that. When you know, you know. A love like that is rare, don't let it slip away without trying," Dante offered. "Take it from someone who knows. Don't let love slip away."

⁕

Juliette tried several times over the following week to call Damian, but she froze every time she dialled his number, unable to hit the call button. He had tried to reach out, sending flowers and texting, asking if she was ok and begging her to let him see her. Juliette wanted to more than anything, but she had felt love's sting before and was scared of feeling it again.

Avery and Dante had told her to go home as she was clearly distracted and grew teary when a newly engaged couple came in to arrange their engagement party. Finally, agreeing that she needed some space, she headed home in a daze.

Milo was home earlier than Juliette expected. He was sitting on the sofa watching a football game when she walked in.

"Have you called him yet?" Milo asked.

"What?" Juliette was shocked; she knew Milo knew about Damian but never expected him to bring it up.

"Mom, I know you are in love with him. You don't have to hide it from me. I also have seen how happy you are when you are around him. Give the guy a chance and call him," Milo smiled softly.

"I'll think about it. I'm going to bed. It's been a long day," Juliette grinned, heading straight to bed without dinner.

⁕

As she drove to the store the next day, Juliette felt a little better and didn't feel so nervous about contacting Damian. Of course, she decided to give herself another day just to be sure. But the fact that her closest friends and colleagues and her son had all offered the same advice, gave her some comfort.

"You can't still be mad at him, can you? Not after this." Avery chirped as Juliette walked in.

On her desk were three bouquets of flowers, each with a note attached. Juliette smiled to herself as she read each single-worded card. I. Love. You. Damian was so thoughtful, and she did appreciate that he hadn't given up on her yet.

"Juliette? The flowers didn't come alone," Dante said.

As Juliette turned around, Dante walked in from the other room hand-in-hand with Cara.

"Sweetheart, what are you doing here? Shouldn't you be in school? Does your Dad know you are here?" Juliette worried.

"I missed you," Cara said sweetly.

"I missed you too. Come here, give me a hug," Juliette enveloped the little girl in a big hug.

Dante mouthed that he would call Damian and let him know his daughter was safe. Juliet smiled and mouthed thank you.

"Daddy is sad. He misses you too. I snook out of school. I wanted to ask you to make Daddy smile again," Cara said innocently.

"Oh, my sweet girl, how are you so cute? Some things adults have to work through themselves. When you are older, you will understand," Juliette grinned. Luckily, the store was along Cara's route from school to home, which relieved some of the panic Juliette felt over Cara's sneaky escapade. Though a very brave escapade.

"I know my Daddy loves you....and I know Mommy scared you."

Juliette looked at Avery, stunned. That was the last thing she expected Cara to say. Children were like sponges. They soaked up everything around them. Like little wheels of information.

"Cara...."

"No, Mommy scares me too. She made Daddy sad too, but not like this. I have never seen him like this before.... I have never seen him smile like he did when he was with you."

Juliette couldn't help it. The look of hope and love in Cara's eyes, mixed with her sweet words, pulled at her. Tears welled in her eyes and she scooped the girl up, holding her tight.

"He is on his way," Dante whispered as he re-entered the room.

Juliette printed off a few colouring pages from the computer and gave Cara a handful of pencils. Then, she sat on the plush pink sofa in her own world, chatting about pirates with Avery while Dante and Juliette waited for Damian to arrive.

As expected, it didn't take Damian long to arrive. He panicked, rushing over to Cara, scooping her in his arms.

"If I didn't love you so much, you would be in so much trouble, young lady. I had the school calling; I was so worried. Why? Why did you run away?" he asked, tears filling his eyes.

"I didn't run away, Daddy. I came to ask Juliette to make you happy again. I miss seeing you smile," Cara said, instantly returning to her drawings when Damian let her go.

Damian and Juliette locked eyes, neither knowing what to say.

"Oh, come on, you guys, this is killing me. Here..." Dante began, grabbing both their hands like they were children and taking them to the sofa on the other side of the store.

"Sit and talk, will you," Dante winked before joining Avery and Cara.

"Thank you for keeping her here. I was so worried."

"You don't need to thank me for that," Juliette smiled. "I would have a word with the principal. What kind of school just allows a child to go missing like that!?"

"Oh, believe me, I will be," Damian smiled, happy that Juliette was talking to him again, even if it wasn't about what they needed to talk about most.

Damian took a deep breath and sighed. Tucking a hair behind her ear, he began to tell his story. Juliette didn't know what to say when he admitted he had cheated in the past, a drunken mistake, when he was very young. She admired his honesty and let him continue. He showed her texts and emails on his phone from Nia. Explaining the break-up, Nia begging for him back, and her raging messages screaming that if she couldn't have him, no one could.

"I'm not going to sit here and claim to be perfect. I have my flaws. Juliette, please at least give me a chance. I'm crazy about you," Damian pleaded.

"I'm crazy about you too," she finally admitted.

Relaxing, Juliette finally believed everything Damian had told her. How could she argue with a paper trail? He wasn't just speaking words she might want to hear; he had proof. Looking into his deep brown eyes, she realized how much she had missed him.

Love isn't meant to be understood. It's meant to be felt. So, I don't need to know what it is about him that makes me feel this way; I just need to embrace it, she told herself.

"So? Can we give this another shot? As an official couple?" Damian asked, trying to suppress his smile.

"I think I'm ok with that," Juliette grinned back.

Damian jumped to his feet, dragging Juliette with him, wrapping his arms around her, and kissing her deeply. Her body came alive with electricity at his touch. She hadn't felt like that since she could remember. Damian was a good man; he was a devoted father and a man not afraid to admit his feelings and flaws. He was a rare kind. And Juliette was glad she had given him a chance.

"Ewww, stop it, that's gross," Avery teased, making everyone laugh.

"Are you back together?" Cara asked excitedly, her face alight with joy.

"Yes, darling, we are," Damian smiled, kissing Juliette softly on the forehead.

Cara ran across the room and wrapped her arms as far around the two of them as she could.

"You are still in trouble for skipping school," Damian joked.

"Hey, you should be thanking her. You two are far too stubborn. If not for this little mischief-maker, lord knows when you two would have seen sense." Dante chuckled.

"See, Daddy, you can't stay mad at me," Cara teased.

☙

Damian and Cara moved into Juliette's house with her and Milo a year later. Milo and Cara clicked instantly, and she loved having an older brother. Milo had taken the role on with open arms.

Milo and Damian got along swimmingly. Damian regularly teased Milo about the first night they met when Milo gave him the 'If you hurt my mother' speech.

Dante and Avery had wondered when Damian would get involved with *Love & Joy*, but Juliette was happy to keep her new love and old separate.

"Who would have thought that a year ago we would be here? To think if Cara hadn't run away from school, who knows where we would be," Juliette said as they unpacked the final box.

"Let's not think of what if and just enjoy the now," Damian smiled, handing Juliette a glass of wine. "A toast. To a year of love and many more to come."

"To Cara," Juliette raised her glass.

"To *Love & Joy*," Damian winked. "The place we first met while organizing the craziest princess pirate party."

Juliette laughed, "It was a crazy party, wasn't it?"

"A crazy day that led to a crazy love-filled romance. I wouldn't change a thing of the past year," Damian said.

"Not even Nia?" Milo piped up as he strode into the kitchen.

"Nope. It took me almost losing your Mother to realize how much she means to me, and I never want to lose her again."

"I love you so much," Juliette smiled, kissing Damian softly.

"Ewww, do we have to see that?" Cara teased.

The kitchen erupted into laughter. This was home. This was family. That was *Love & Joy*.

The End

Something Borrowed

THE WEDDING TRIO BOOK 2

$O_{n\varepsilon}$

AVERY SAT on the edge of the bed, looking at the closet and the chaos that was once the bedroom she shared with Gemma. Coat hangers lay discarded on the floor. Drawers slanted, impossible to close. The whole place was a mess. Avery let her tears fall. How had everything fallen apart so quickly? Gemma and Avery always had issues, but didn't everyone? Wasn't a small amount of conflict what kept life interesting? It kept the mind sharp and brought what was important into focus. That's what Avery had always told herself anyway.

Her wedding dress lay crumpled in the corner on the floor. Gemma had no regard for Avery's feelings when she'd discarded the dress so callously. Looking over at the nightstand, Avery caught a glimpse of the gold photo frame of her wedding day. Gemma and Avery in matching dresses stood side by side. It was taken only three years ago. When did it all go wrong?

She wondered if it had anything to do with the struggle they'd had trying to adopt their daughter, Emma. Being not only a same-sex couple but with one mother being trans-gender, it had been difficult. But Avery and Gemma never let that stop them. They pushed on, comforting each other through each rejection and celebrating with each piece of good news. Every tear had been worth it when they'd brought their little bundle of joy home.

"It was meant to be. A child who needed to be loved, finding a home with so much love to give," Gemma had said.

Thinking back to that day tore Avery's heart. Was it her or the baby that Gemma had issues with? Avery didn't want to give it a second thought. She had known Gemma had been unhappy for a while but assumed it was nothing more than her adjusting to her new life as a mother. Everything had been so beautiful, but once the novelty of a new baby wore off and responsibility kicked in, Gemma seemed to crumble.

She hadn't coped well with the sleepless nights and never knew how to handle Emma when she cried seemingly for no reason. She'd missed her old life of partying and freedom too much. When they argued one evening and Gemma threatened to leave, Avery never thought Gemma had meant it. *Just angry words meant to hurt,* she told herself. Little did Avery know just how much those words could hurt until she came home from a day out with Emma to find Gemma had packed her things and gone. No note, no explanation, nothing.

Emma crying from her bassinet in the living room broke Avery out of her self-pity. She didn't have the time to spill tears over someone who didn't deserve them. She had someone far more important to worry about. Her daughter needed her. Striding into the living room, Avery wiped away her tears and scooped up her beautiful four-month-old with a head full of dark curly hair and stunning emerald-green eyes. Looking at her child's face made her pain and worries melt away.

Emma had brought a new kind of love into Avery's life, a love like no other. She was a beacon of pure light. Avery would melt whenever she held her. When Emma looked up, and her lips creased into the closest thing to a smile a baby could manage, it was as though a light came on in the world. As long as she had Emma in her life, all was good and well.

"Don't you worry, baby, mommy is here. Everything will be okay," Avery said, swaying with Emma back and forth.

After giving Emma her bottle and putting her back to sleep, Avery had a small glass of wine to calm her nerves. Looking in the mirror, she gave herself a pep talk that she had memorized over the years.

You have fought through worse than this. You have come back from worse than this. You deserve love, and you are love. You are strong. You are beautiful, and the world is yours for the taking. It's ok to cry and be sad, but once you have cried your river, it's time to get back on the horse and slay.

It did the trick every time. With her pep talk ringing in her ears, Avery began to pick up the mess Gemma had left behind, boxing up old memories that only brought hurt and pain. She would call it a spring cleaning. Tidying up always helped Avery clear her mind. *Clearing out the negative energy only leaves room for the positive,* she told herself.

As the weeks went by, Avery thought that she was coping well until, one morning, she woke up to find a large yellow envelope waiting for her in the mailbox. She discarded it on the dining table, concentrating instead on fussing over Emma; she was in need of a diaper change. Envelopes like that never carried good news, and Avery was afraid of what might be inside. She busied herself with the task of settling the baby, fussing over little details that could probably be left for later. But the envelope screamed at her every time she caught a glimpse of it or passed by the table as she straightened the room. Eventually, she decided enough was enough. How bad could it be?

"Divorce papers?" Avery yelled, her voice waking Emma so that the baby cried. "She filed for divorce?"

A small part of Avery always thought Gemma would come back. That her act of rebellion was just her version of a mid-life crisis, and once it was out of her system, they would be a family again. As the large black letters stared back at her from the page, she felt the world around her crumble.

Avery was never one for self-pity, so she decided enough was enough. After a week of not leaving the house, it was time to take positive action. It wasn't just Gemma leaving that had left her feeling unsettled. It was the world around her. Her neighbours hadn't been the nicest when Gemma and Avery moved in. And she was tired of the general feel of the neighbourhood. Gemma's friends had become her friends, so she had no one when Gemma left. Apart from Emma, nothing was keeping her in that town anymore. She had only moved there because Gemma wanted to, Avery would have been happy to say in

Seattle. She didn't want Emma to be raised in a place that no longer held any love. What she needed was a new home. A fresh start.

It didn't take her long to find the small town called Summershore; a small town in the hills of California. It was perfect. It had a lovely lake, scenic views, and everything that Avery missed about home. Summershore called to her. With Emma on her hip, she left three days later to view a small little house she had spotted online.

Seeing it in person, Avery instantly fell in love. The picture didn't do the house justice. It was a cute two-storey building with a tiny front porch just big enough for a small porch swing. It had a dark grey door and roof, giving the house a cosy feel. The door opened up right into the living room. It had a cute cottage-style kitchen and two small bedrooms. It was just big enough for Avery and Emma.

"What do you think, sweetie? Is this the house for us?" Avery asked Emma.

Emma blinked back, not understanding the question, but Avery never honestly expected an answer.

She smiled at the realtor. "We'll take it!"

Her next adventure had begun.

Two

AFTER SETTING herself and Emma up in their new home, Avery spent a day strolling around Summershore in the afternoon sun, getting acquainted with her new hometown. Avery fell more in love with each welcoming hello, friendly smile, and scenic view and knew that Summershore would be the best home for herself and Emma.

"I think this place will be perfect for us," Avery rocked Emma to sleep on the porch swing. "But there is only so long I can chill. Mommy's got to get herself a job to give you all the best things in life."

Settling Emma down after her bottle, Avery loaded up her laptop, printed off some fresh copies of her resume, and began searching for job openings online. Many good jobs were just outside of Summershore, but the working hours would have been a conflict for a single mother. She needed a job with sociable hours, good pay, and something close to home to be there for Emma when she needed her. After several hours of searching, she submitted several applications. To her delight, she was able to set up several interviews over the next few days.

First was a marketing assistant position at Summershore's biggest marketing company. But they went with a candidate that had a little more knowledge of the area than Avery. She appreciated their communication. It vexed Avery when companies said that they would be in touch and then never followed through. Waiting was the worst. Her following interview was for a sales associate, and her third was for a catering assistant – Avery had always had a talent when it came to creating delicious meals in the kitchen.

After several weeks, Avery's confidence took a hit. While some interviews went well, nothing ever came of them, and others never even gave her a chance. She didn't want to think about why they rejected her, but based on her experience, she knew not everyone was open-minded when they realised she was trans, or compassionate to her needs as a new mother. As discouraging as it was, Avery had a thick skin and wouldn't let people get to her like that. Every morning before she left for another interview, she gave herself a pep talk, practised her power poses from her favourite positive mindset books and went out ready to take on the world.

"Crap, my savings hasn't taken a hit like this in years," she mumbled at the ATM as she withdrew funds to buy groceries.

After several weeks and no real sign of a job on the horizon, Avery began to panic. She had enough savings to last a bit longer, but she didn't want to rely on that. Her savings were dwindling quickly, and she had no idea what she would do once those funds ran out.

Avery headed to The Golden Coffee Bean to grab an iced Frappuccino where she came across a notice board. Scanning through the listings, she noticed several postings for jobs in the area. Some were less than ideal, with part-time hours or minimum wage. At this point, she decided she couldn't be picky. A job was a job, after all. One listing stuck out more than most. The poster was beautiful, and when she pulled off the tab with the contact details, butterflies fluttered in her stomach.

"*Love & Joy*, how cute," Avery murmured as she examined the logo at the top of the poster.

Avery sipped her Frappuccino and began to make calls, sitting outside where she could draw positive energy from the view of the lake and the rolling hills beyond. One vacancy had already been filled, and another had wrapped up the interview stage. She left *Love & Joy* until last. She didn't have a lot of management experience, but she thought the worst thing that could happen would be for them to say no. If she didn't try, what was she going to do? Sit around and wonder what might have happened?

Someone picked up on the first ring. "Good afternoon, Love & Joy Wedding and Event Planning. Dante speaking, how may I help you?" came a deep melodic voice.

"Hi, my name is Avery Lannister. I came across your advertisement for an assistant manager. Is the position still open?"

"Of course, of course. Do you have a pen? I'll give you our email address. Send over a copy of your resume and a cover letter detailing a little about yourself, and I will get back to you ASAP. We are scheduling interviews shortly, so the quicker you send it, the better. I'm not going to lie. We have had a lot of applicants so far," Dante replied.

Avery thanked him and jotted down the email on the napkin that came with her croissant. Not wanting to waste a second, she hung up and headed home with Emma to apply.

Three days later, Avery sat with her morning coffee on the front porch feeling defeated. She had no interviews lined up and debated applying for jobs outside of Summershore. She didn't want to hire a nanny to raise Emma, but what choice would she have if a job didn't present itself? A stray tear rolled down her cheek just as her phone rang. Wiping away her tear, she picked up her phone. It was a number she didn't recognize, but it was a local area code calling, from what she could tell. *A job?*

Her hands shook in anticipation making it hard to hit the button to accept the call. "Hello?"

"Hi, is this Avery Lannister?"

"It sure is. How can I help you?"

"It's Dante, from *Love & Joy*. You applied for the assistant manager position. While you don't have much management experience, your resume is impressive, and I'd love to invite you in for an interview." The happiness in Dante's voice was infectious, instantly lifting Avery's mood.

"Oh my god, thank you so much. When would you like me to come in?"

"Is Thursday or Friday better for you?"

"Friday gives me enough time to find a babysitter."

"Perfect, I will email you all the details. I look forward to meeting you. Enjoy your day." Dante ended the call.

Ecstatic, Avery jumped up and spent the next few hours hunting for a babysitter and planning her outfit, makeup, and shoes. She even spent time practising her interview skills in the bedroom mirror. She had an excellent feeling about *Love & Joy*, a feeling she hadn't had for a long time.

Friday rolled around. Her interview was scheduled for late afternoon, giving her enough time to get through her to-do list and care for Emma. Avery was ready to go, settling for a black power suit with a white and red polka dot shirt. Checking her watch, she began to worry that she would be late for the interview if her babysitter didn't turn up soon. First impressions were everything, and she didn't want to miss an excellent opportunity. Picking up her phone, she dialled the number for the agency she booked her babysitter through. Straight away, they patched her through to the young girl's phone.

"Hi, is this Stephanie? I have a booking with you to watch Emma for a couple of hours? I'm due to leave any minute. I was just wondering, what is your ETA?" Avery asked, trying to keep the nerves from her voice.

"I'm so sorry; I lost your number. I meant to call sooner. I won't be able to make it, something has come up at home, and I have to cancel all of my afternoon appointments," the girl replied and ended the call before Avery could even speak.

"Are you kidding? How unprofessional," Avery snapped, shoving her phone into her handbag.

Checking her watch, she had to think fast. If she didn't leave within five minutes, she wouldn't make it across town during rush hour traffic.

"Looks like you're coming with me," Avery smiled, scooping up Emma and heading to the car.

She arrived at *Love & Joy* with minutes to spare. Pulling her frontal baby carrier from the trunk, she strapped Emma to her chest, repeated her pep talk in her head, and strolled into the store with as much confidence as she could muster.

Three

A SMALL BELL rang above her head as she entered *Love & Joy*. Looking at the store, Avery was awestruck. It was beautiful, decorated in shades of pink and pale blue. A large canvas sat on the back wall behind the main desk depicting a wedding day and a couple with a baby boy in their arms. Flowers sat on every table, the scent a delight to the senses. Avery felt her skin break out into goosebumps like it did when she first saw her new home.

A tall, dark, handsome, and very well-dressed man greeted her with a warm and welcoming smile. He had impeccable style, and Avery couldn't help but admire him.

"Hello, how can we help you? Are you here to organize a party for this little darling?" he asked, stroking Emma on the cheek. He shook her hand and led her over to the small area with 'Consultation' written in gold calligraphy on the wall.

"No, actually, I'm here for the interview. I'm Avery Lannister. I'm so sorry my babysitter cancelled last minute, and I didn't want to miss such a wonderful opportunity," Avery smiled nervously, sitting down and unbuckling Emma's carrier.

"Not a problem at all, would you like a drink?" offered a tall blonde-haired beauty as she joined them from the other side of the room. Avery had caught a glimpse of the woman's picture around the store when she entered, quickly realizing she was Juliette, the owner.

Avery smiled. "No, thank you."

She didn't know if it was the beauty of the story, the goosebumps she felt when she walked in, or the welcoming atmosphere, but she felt instantly at ease as they told her a little about what they did at *Love & Joy*. She got a feeling of being home and knew in her heart that she could be herself with them. She decided honesty was the best policy and explained that while she didn't have much experience, she was a quick study and always willing to learn. She listed her prior experience in sales and customer service.

"I'm looking for a job that will allow me the freedom to still have a hand in raising my daughter.... I don't want her to be raised by a nanny." This was the deal-breaker, and she knew it. Not many companies would be so understanding of this goal. Avery sat waiting, her heart pounding at the surprise on their faces.

The surprise didn't last before their faces broke into smiles, instantly putting Avery at ease. After the standard interview questions, Dante excused himself to check on Avery's references leaving her and Juliette to talk. Juliette was so open and kind that Avery felt free to tell her story. She gave her a brief outline of how she and Gemma adopted Emma and how Gemma left. She didn't feel the need to hide the fact she was transgender and appreciated how Juliette listened and took it all in. Juliette was a mother herself, so she understood Avery's need to be in her daughter's life, not wanting to miss out on the milestones.

"I hear you. Thank you for sharing your story," Juliette smiled, placing a comforting hand on Avery's knee. "So is Avery your legal name...did you..."

Avery smiled sweetly, she could tell Juliette was a caring person and didn't want to upset or offend her, but these questions need to be asked when filling out the documentation for hiring someone new. She had to do what was right for her business.

"It's okay, you can ask. Avery is my birth name. It was like my parents knew I would need a gender-neutral name later on in life."

Juliette beamed. "That's beautiful. I love that."

Dante re-joined them. The rest of the interview didn't last much longer before Dante and Juliette, after a quick consultation, offered Avery the job on the spot. Overjoyed, Avery had to stop herself from crying tears of joy. She was so excited that she didn't want to wait until the following week and insisted she could start right away.

Juliette agreed that Avery was more than welcome to bring Emma into the office with her if a babysitter wasn't possible, making Avery even happier. She was super grateful for her understanding and wanted to thank her by doing the best job she possibly could. Avery felt like she fit into the team instantly. It was like she was meant to find *Love & Joy* in order to restore the love and joy in her own life.

Juliette and Dante gave Avery a list of responsibilities to choose from. Given that she didn't have much experience, they didn't want to overwhelm her with tasks she couldn't handle. With her sales and customer service background, Avery jumped at the chance to manage the new client accounts and took over opening the newly extended part of the store. She worked closely with decorators, builders, and the planning department to get the best deals and the quickest completion dates. Dante and Juliette were never shy in telling her how impressed they were with her work. In no time at all, the *Love & Joy* team felt like a family, leaving Juliette to go home every night with a smile on her face to the point her cheeks hurt.

The family feel was extended to Emma, too. The clients loved that while *Love & Joy* was a business, family always came first. But what surprised and warmed Avery's heart the most was how Milo – Juliette's son – had naturally fallen into the role of Emma's babysitter. He was wonderful with her, and as the months went by, he adopted the role of big brother. It was beautiful. Avery couldn't remember a time when she was so happy.

Love & Joy gave Avery the perfect work-life balance. On the days when she knew she needed a break, she could work from home and hire a babysitter to help with Emma while still having a hand in her day-to-day life. She grew close to Dante and Juliette, and with the help of Milo, she was able to go out and make new friends in Summershore.

Four

"HEY GUYS, GUESS WHAT?" Avery cheered after ending her phone call.

"What's up?" Dante asked.

"The speed dating event I'm organizing for *Love Online* just called, and they said it's proving to be even bigger than expected. They have a few open slots and asked if any of the team wanted to join. I said I would ask and get back to them. What do you think? I'm game. Who else?" Avery asked.

"It might be fun. Sign me up!" Dante shouted, already hyper about the idea.

"I don't know," Juliette mumbled.

"Oh, go on, Mom. It will be fun," Milo interjected

"Exactly, it will be fun. We don't even have to take it too seriously. I'm not looking for anything serious right now, but who wouldn't want to be wined and dined and treated to a date every once in a while?" Avery spoke up, trying to convince Juliette.

"I'm just not ready for that kind of thing."

"I'm signing you up. You never know. You might change your mind and enjoy it," Avery told Juliette, jumping back to her desk, and typing the email reply.

The speed dating event wasn't for another few weeks, but Dante and Avery grew more and more excited as it drew closer. They spent days shopping for outfits and gossiping over their morning coffee about what their perfect partner would look like.

"I want tall, but not too tall. He can't be taller than me. Blonde with blue eyes. I'm partial to a tattoo. Sweet, sensitive, but also tough and manly...." Dante was positively swooning.

"You don't want much, do you?" Avery joked, shaking her head at his list of must-haves.

"I have high standards, darling. Have you seen this prize?" Dante asked, giving a mock twirl. "This king deserves a king!" Dante laughed.

Avery couldn't argue. Dante was one of a kind. He was kind, sweet, funny, and one of the most intelligent people Avery had ever met. He had a skill with people, reading them better than they could read themselves. He was terrific with Emma and was always able to cheer everyone up. The room lit up every time he walked in. He was a positive ray of sunshine that everyone needed in their lives.

"What about you?" Dante asked.

"I just want someone I have something in common with but is still their own person. Obviously, someone good with kids, who will be good for Emma and me."

"Can you be a bit more specific?" Dante enquired.

"I honestly haven't given it much thought. I thought I knew what I wanted with Gemma, but now, I'm not overthinking it and just want to let love find me," Avery answered.

The speed dating event finally rolled around. And thanks to a little helpful probing from Milo, Juliette agreed to join them. Dante jumped at the opportunity to give everyone a makeover, and the night was, all in all, a huge success. It had been set up as a networking event and a way for *Love Online* to launch itself to the public. Avery loved people-watching, and she loved watching all the singles couple up. She could tell when someone was trying to hide the fact that they liked the person in front of them. She knew Juliette wasn't entirely on board with the event, so she tried to keep a close eye on her. At least that was the plan until Steve sat down.

"Hi, I'm Steve. What's your name?"

"Avery." She offered her hand to shake.

Avery believed you could tell a lot about someone by their hand-shake, and Steve's was strong, firm, but tender. He was a little shorter than Avery but took care of himself. He was stylish and had dreamy brown eyes that Avery felt she could get lost in.

Out of all the people she chatted with at the event, Steve was the only one to leave a real impression. At the end of the event, Avery, Juliette, and Dante chatted at the bar, comparing their experiences.

"Thank you so much for convincing me to come tonight. I had a lot of fun," Juliette said, accepting her cosmopolitan cocktail from the bartender.

"Did anyone catch your eye?" Avery asked.

"No, I didn't feel that spark, but it has opened my eyes. I'm ready for new love. But I'm taking a leaf from your book Avery. I'm going to let love find me." Juliette smiled, clicking her cocktail glass with Avery's

"Yes, girl. I'm so happy for you!" Avery couldn't have hoped for more. Her beautiful boss had been grieving for too long. She turned towards Dante, anxious to find out his impressions of the event. "So Dante, tell us about that yummy piece of man-candy we had to drag you away from," Avery teased.

"His name is David, but I'm calling him Dave. He's cool with it. He is a dentist and fine as hell," Dante gushed, making the group laugh.

"What about you?" Juliette asked, poking Avery in the shoulder.

Avery laughed, noting how tipsy Juliette was getting. She had been so tense for months. It warmed Avery's heart to see her finally relax and let her hair down. Juliette wasn't just her boss. She had become a close friend who Avery cared for a lot.

"Excuse me?" interrupted Steve tapping Avery on the shoulder before she could answer Juliette.

"Oh hey, Steve, what's up?"

"I had a lot of fun tonight, but I had the most fun in the five minutes I spent with you. Here is my cell. call me sometime." Steve winked, placing a soft, gentle kiss on Avery's cheek before excusing himself to re-join his group of friends at the other side of the bar.

"Oh, my god, girl!" Juliette cheered.

Steve and Avery went on a few dates. He was a barista at *The Golden Coffee Bean* and joked how he had served Avery many times, but she had never noticed him. He made Avery laugh so much her sides hurt. Sadly, after date three, it became apparent that while they had fun together, they were not a good fit. They ended their dating streak amicably and agreed to stay friends. Avery never believed a word of it. In her experience, anyone who said they wanted to 'stay friends' generally disappeared completely after a month or two. However, Steve proved to be different, and even months later, they were still good friends.

"Hey Avery, are you still dating?" Steve asked one morning when Avery came to collect *Love & Joy*'s coffee order.

"No one is in the cards. Why?"

"I may have found someone who is perfect for you. Her name is Emily. Is it cool if I give her your number?"

"I don't know. I don't do blind dates," Avery hedged.

"Oh, come on. You trust me, right? Look," Steve pulled out his phone and brought up a picture of Emily.

She was cute, a short, redheaded girl with green eyes, high cheekbones, and a butterfly tattoo on her collar bone.

"Ok, fine, get her to call me," Avery reluctantly agreed with a cheeky smile. She gave Steve a quick peck on the cheek, she collected the coffee and headed out, telling herself she wasn't getting her hopes up over a blind date.

Emily turned out to be fun, but there was an age gap that Avery couldn't get past. Emily was five years younger than Avery and was still finding her place in the world. She came on a bit too strong, constantly texting and calling when Avery didn't reply right away. It was a little too much to take sometimes. Emma was always the priority for Avery, and Emily was not someone Avery thought would be a good fit in her daughter's life.

"How's dating life going?" Dante asked, after a week or two.

"I'm cooling dating for a while. Steve was nice, but we are better as friends, and Emily was just.... wow, she's sweet, but she's still a kid and isn't ready for an adult relationship. I'm just going to concentrate on Emma and work for the time being."

"Oh, sweetie," Dante hugged Avery, giving her a sympathetic look.

"It's fine. Honestly." Avery really was speaking the truth. Dating wasn't something she was ready for yet.

Not long after the dating event, Juliette met Damian, a handsome single father wanting a party for his little girl. Dante and Avery had comforted Juliette when Damian's toxic ex-girlfriend came back on the scene trying to break up their relationship. After such a rocky start, it was a pleasure to see how their relationship blossomed and strengthened after that.

Watching Dante and David's relationship develop and noticing how Juliette received so many flowers from Damian at the office, Avery was surrounded with more love than ever. Usually, she would be happy with that, but it slowly began to feel suffocating. She would go home every night alone, longing for what her friends had. But the idea of dating and opening up to someone new terrified her. That kind of relationship meant opening up about her past, and she really wasn't ready to go there again. She still had to stop herself from messaging Gemma several times a day, even though Avery knew it was a bad idea.

No, she wanted someone to share her highs and lows with. Someone who she could grow with. She missed cuddling up on the sofa, watching movies, and making plans for the future. She wasn't lonely exactly. She simply missed having that special connection with someone who saw you in a world where it was easy to get lost in the crowd.

Five

AVERY APPRECIATED HOW MUCH DANTE, Juliette, and Milo cared for her and seemed to notice when she wasn't herself. She held back though from telling them what she'd been thinking lately. Until she figured out what she wanted, she decided to play her cards close to her chest.

Love & Joy helped organize several LGBTQ+ events, and Avery was a huge part of a stunning Valentine's Day double wedding for twin brothers who married two best friends. The brides celebrated officially becoming sisters, and the couples held so much love for each other, it was dazzling. When Avery got home after the wedding, she curled up in bed with a cup of hot chocolate and loaded up *Love Online*. Working on the speed dating event had given Avery confidence in the site, so she signed up for online dating.

Avery had never tried online dating before. She found as her inbox filled with message requests, it gave her a slight sense of validation. It was a small confidence boost that she didn't know she needed. Unfortunately, most of the messages were anticlimactic. A few started with the standard *'Hi, how are you? You're hot!'* but no replies after that. A few were far too forward or demanding. She even received the odd inappropriate picture. From the tons of messages she received, only a handful resulted in any genuine conversation, and even fewer resulted in actual dates.

One date she went on was with a woman named Samantha. But when she found out that Avery had a daughter, Samantha clammed up. When Avery got home, she found Samantha had blocked her number. The next date she went on was with Eva, who was far too self-obsessed for Avery's liking. Hoping for the third time lucky, Avery agreed to go on a date with Chelsea. The conversation had flowed freely online, but it was stunted and dry in person. The evening seemed to last forever, with many awkward minutes of silence and dead-end conversations.

After all her bad luck on the dating scene, self-doubt began to creep in. She couldn't take the highs and lows. It was like a rollercoaster. The excitement of meeting someone new, the nerves about opening up, and the lows when they ghosted or blocked her were exhausting.

Online dating is not for me.

Cancelling her membership to *Love Online*, Avery closed her laptop and went to bed, but sleep didn't come easy. For the first time since the night Gemma left, her bed had never felt so empty.

The following day, Avery allowed herself to slip into a place of self-pity to the point where she couldn't even find the will to give herself her morning pep talk. Dante had texted asking if she could pick up the team's coffees while he headed out of town for a meeting about the extension of the business. Avery agreed and called her babysitter to take Emma for the day. She didn't want Emma to pick up on her bad mood. Once the sitter arrived, Avery kissed Emma goodbye and drove down to The Golden Coffee Bean.

She was struggling to carry the large order. Avery had just made it back to her car when she heard a woman groaning and complaining. Curiosity took hold, and Avery looked around, searching for the location of the commotion.

"Stupid piece of crap!" yelled a tall brunette as she kicked her car tire.

Avery knew a little about cars. Gemma had been a mechanic, bikes being her thing, but Avery had picked up a thing or two over the years. The car's hood was open, and a heap of steam poured out. The woman crouched on the ground in front of her broken-down car with her face in her hands.

Her beauty instantly struck Avery. Large, almond-shaped brown eyes, high cheekbones, and a sharp jawline gave the stranger an exotic beauty. She had a full sleeve tattoo on her left arm, a nose ring, and her eyebrow was pierced. She gave off a rock chick vibe that Avery loved.

"Need a hand?" Avery asked.

The woman jumped, not realising Avery was standing by. Jumping to her feet, she brushed off her clothes which were covered in paint spatter.

"You don't happen to know anything about piece of crap cars, do you?" she asked.

Avery laughed. "I do, actually."

Avery moved to check the engine and dropped to the ground to confirm her suspicions. Looking under the car, she saw what she needed to know. Brushing herself off, she stood up and turned to the annoyed rock chick.

"Do you want the good news or the bad news?" Avery asked.

"Good news. Always start with good news."

"I'm friends with the guy who owns the auto shop and can help you out with a deal to get this fixed."

"And the bad news?"

"Your radiator is busted. Even with a friend's discount, it will be pricey," Avery offered.

The rock chick sighed and ran her hands through her hair, kicking her tire a few more times in frustration. When she was done, she glanced over at Avery with a rueful look. "Right, all the anger is out now. Thanks for your help. I'm not going to lie. I didn't expect someone as glamorous as you to know anything about cars."

"Looks can be deceiving." Avery smiled.

"So, if you are helping me out with a friend's discount at the auto shop, it's only fair you know my name. Hi, I'm Sarah." She smiled, offering a paint and ink-covered hand to shake.

When their hands met, Avery felt her skin tingle all the way up to her elbow, "Avery." She smiled back, hoping like crazy that her interest in the other woman was obvious.

Avery called Frank at the auto shop and agreed to wait with Sarah until the tow truck arrived. She enjoyed her company. They made small talk, laughed, and joked, and Sarah flirted a lot. Avery was surprised by how much she blushed and didn't know how to react. Everything with Sarah felt so natural like they had known each other for years. When Frank came, he agreed to offer Sarah a fifteen percent discount on her repairs.

"So, how much more flirting do I need to do before you ask me for my number?" Sarah asked with a wink.

Stunned, Avery fell silent, almost dropping her phone.

"Tell you what, how about I give you mine?" Sarah chuckled, taking Avery's phone from her hand, and saving her number for her.

She hit dial and saved Avery's number in return. Winking back at her as she climbed into the truck alongside Frank and headed off to get her car fixed, leaving Avery to head back to *Love & Joy* with an ear-to-ear smile on her face.

"You're late. Everything okay with Emma?" Juliette asked, grabbing the coffee tray off Avery before she dropped it all.

"Yeah, sorry, I.... bumped into someone. Her car had broken down, and I waited until Frank came," Avery answered.

"You met someone?" Juliette chimed.

"No."

"Did you exchange numbers?"

Avery blushed, causing Juliette to chuckle softly.

"Good for you, love," she said and smiled.

Six

AVERY CHOSE to keep Sarah her little secret for now. She wanted to find out if it would develop into something before revealing anything to her friends. The day after Sarah's car broke down, she waited outside *The Golden Coffee Bean*, hoping to bump into Avery. Avery couldn't help but smile when she saw Sarah outside holding a bouquet of flowers in one hand, a cup of coffee in the other.

Sarah smiled. "Morning, I was hoping to run into you here."

"Everything okay with your car?"

"It's going to be a day or two, but yes. I wanted to thank you in person. It's so impersonal over text. You didn't have to help me, and I appreciated it," Sarah said, handing Avery the flowers.

"Oh, you didn't need to do that. I was happy to help. We girls have to stick together, right?"

After chatting a little longer, they both went about their day. Sarah kept Avery pleasantly distracted with cute texts throughout the day, and within a week, a date was arranged. For the first time in a long time, Avery wasn't dreading the first date. She liked Sarah and looked forward to getting to know her better.

"Milo, can I ask a favour?"

"Sure, Avery," Milo answered.

"I have a date tomorrow night, but I want to keep it on the DL. Are you okay babysitting Emma for a while? I'll pay you, of course."

"You don't need to pay me. You're family." Milo grinned and winked. "And don't worry. Your secret is safe with me."

⁂

Sarah and Avery arranged to go to a cocktail bar outside Summershore called *Straws and Umbrellas*. It was a hip little spot paying homage to '90s pop culture. Avery opted for a black and red floral, V-neck cocktail dress, and killer red high heels. She sat at the bar nervously waiting, nursing her vodka martini, until she saw Sarah walk in. Sarah looked beautiful in red and black plaid cigarette pants with a black studded belt. She wore a black lace bodysuit underneath, a black cropped leather jacket, and black suede platform heels that elongated her stunning legs.

"Wow, now I feel overdressed." Avery smiled, climbing down from her stool to hug Sarah.

"You look stunning," Sarah replied, kissing Avery on both cheeks, in a way that felt foreign and exotic, but very right.

Sarah ordered a beer, and instantly, the night flowed beautifully. They got along like old friends. It should have been perfect, but Avery still held a small part of herself back. She wanted to know how serious Sarah was about dating before opening up. Was this a casual thing or something more?

They discussed music, movies, food, fashion, work, and other first-date lines of conversation before Sarah decided to take the lead. "So now all the fun chat is out the way, let's get serious," Sarah said, ordering another round of drinks.

"You first," Avery said nervously.

"Ok. Well, I was born and raised in New York. I lived there all my life. I started my graffiti art career at a modern art gallery called G-A-Art. I worked there for...three years. After a major art show, probably the biggest in the gallery's history, since they were fairly new when I joined, things changed."

"How so?"

"Money grew tight, and the owner decided to stop paying me for my work. I agreed at first, believing all his lies about it just being a bump in the road. I started spending my own money on promotions, supplies, everything. Eventually, I called him on his crap and when he got angry, I left. I tried opening my own gallery. I even tried joining others, but he had connections and started derailing my career."

Avery gasped. "That's terrible!"

"It's all good. That's when I moved here. Best move I ever made. I have my own studio here, and my art is selling in galleries here, in neighbouring towns, and online." Sarah smiled.

"That explains all the paint and ink the first day we met," Avery joked.

"I can show you my studio later tonight if you like," Sarah mentioned, a spark of excitement in her eyes as she waited for Avery's response.

"That would be great. I'd love to see it."

Hearing about Sarah's issues and what made her move from her beloved New York to Summershore, Avery decided to share her story, or at least a small part of it anyway. Avery didn't like to admit it, but she had a hard time trusting people. It took her a while to allow herself to be truly vulnerable with someone.

"I moved to Summershore not long ago. Emma was only four months old. She's now almost one now. Wow.... Where has that time gone?" Avery wondered and shook her head.

"Emma?"

"My daughter." Avery paused, watching Sarah closely. How would she react?

Sarah grinned back; sensing Avery was guarded, she waited for her to continue at her own pace. Opening up, Avery explained the troubles she and Gemma had finding the right adoption agency, and bringing Emma home. She told her how things had changed between them then, and how she had come home one day to find Gemma had up and left.

"That sucks. It's her loss because I think you are amazing," Sarah offered.

"Thanks." Avery shrugged. "After she left, she filed for divorce with no warning. It was the final straw. Once everything was finalised and I realised that Gemma had given full custody of Emma over to me, I packed up and moved here. It was the best thing I could possibly have done because that's when I found *Love & Joy*."

"Who are they?"

Avery laughed and explained the business and how Dante, Juliette, and Milo had accepted her and brought her and Emma into their family. She sang their praises and made a mental note to remind them how much she appreciated their constant love and support. When she finally stopped, she looked up to find Sarah beaming at her.

"You speak about them with so much passion and love. It's beautiful."

Finishing their drinks, they headed out to call a cab. Sarah took Avery to her studio tucked in the hills overlooking the lake with a breathtaking view of the Summershore skyline. One wall housed floor-to-ceiling windows, and the other three were painted with a mix of graffiti art. One wall depicted the sunset over the skyline, and the others looked like a visual representation of all of Sarah's emotions. It was raw and vulnerable and beautiful.

Avery felt honoured that Sarah was showing this to her. She talked her through her latest pieces and showed her a large canvas she was getting ready to ship. Before the night ended, Sarah handed Avery a small canvas. When she opened the brown protective paper, Avery was stunned. Inside was a picture of her in front of Sarah's broken-down car, only Avery was dressed as a valiant warrior. In small writing across the top, it was the words, *'My knight in shining armour.'*

"Sarah, this is.... wow.... I can't thank you enough. It's beautiful. No one has ever done anything like this for me," Avery said, overwhelmed with emotion by such a beautiful and heartfelt gesture.

"You could give me a good night kiss," Sarah suggested and winked.

Seven

THE FOLLOWING MORNING, Avery arrived at *Love & Joy* with a spring in her step. As she worked, she sang along with the radio in the office a little louder than usual. Her excitement ran over into every aspect of her life. She was more enthusiastic with each event she helped organize. Dante and Juliette both enquired as to what had her so giddy, but with it being early days with Sarah, she kept her mouth closed. Only Milo truly knew the reason for the lift in her mood.

"So, how are things going with you and Damian? He seems to be a permanent fixture around this place," Avery said, eager for a change of subject before she spilled the beans about her date with Sarah.

"Wonderful," Juliette sighed.

"They are talking about moving in together," Milo offered.

"No way! Juliette, that amazing," Dante chirped, clapping his hands in applause at the announcement.

"I think it's a cause for after-work celebration drinks," Avery cheered, in the mood for celebration already.

Juliette laughed and agreed. After all the issues with Nia trying to cause conflict and almost splitting Juliette and Damian up, it was nice to see they were making moves in the right direction.

"What about David?" Avery swivelled her desk chair to ask Dante.

"Dave!" Dante jokingly snapped. He had grown quite attached to the shortened version of his new beau's name. "Things are going well. We're having fun, but you know me. I'm too old for all that lovey-dovey stuff."

Avery laughed. "Lovey-dovey stuff? Dante, you work for a wedding planner."

"It's nice planning it for *others*. I'm just enjoying things with Dave as they are," Dante offered, clearly not wanting to go into much detail.

Avery respected that. She wasn't willing to push the issue, especially since she wasn't willing to open up about Sarah yet herself.

Leaving the relationship talk behind, the conversation swiftly shifted back to business. With Avery and Dante both working hard, the company was running smoothly. The expansion had been a success; giving more space for different events while separating corporate from personal events. Avery bit her lip as she considered voicing an idea that had been on her mind more and more lately. As she looked over the accounts and saw how business was progressing and the ever-growing waiting list of clients, she knew it was time to speak up.

"Juliette, have you ever thought of franchising the business? Venturing out into the big cities? With the way business is booming, you could do that in a year or two," Avery offered.

"Wow, do you really think so?" Juliette asked, surprised.

"Of course, it would bring in a whole new revenue line, and you could spread your brand of *Love & Joy* further afield. Who knows, in the next ten years, there could be a *Love & Joy* in every state."

Juliette's expression was a mix of surprise and horror. Avery worried that she had overstepped herself. She was so enthusiastic about the business and her friend's success that she wanted to help out more, just as Dante had. The company's first expansion was his idea, and Juliette had welcomed it with open arms. A thought occurred to Avery that maybe if she were better prepared and offered Juliette her ideas with a solid business plan as Dante had, then perhaps her ideas would be taken seriously.

Juliette laughed nervously. "Slow down, Avery!"

Avery nodded, chastened. She'd definitely gone about it all wrong. "I'm sorry. I didn't mean to overstep."

"No, no, sweetie, you haven't. It's just a little scary thinking about it, that's all. But I will give your ideas some thought. I love how you and Dante care about the future of the business. It means a lot." Juliette smiled.

Eight

THE WONDERFUL THING about Sarah being a graffiti artist meant that she had the freedom to make her own hours. So, over the following months, they worked date night around Avery's schedule. They enjoyed trying new things, so they changed it up each week. Sailing on the lake, horseback riding in the hills, art classes – more for Sarah to show off her skills – pottery classes, cooking classes, the regular dinner and drinks, and the occasional movie.

The closer Sarah and Avery became, the harder it became for Avery to say goodnight. She found each time the date ended, she was left feeling deflated, wanting more. She missed her when she was gone and couldn't wait to see her again. Finally realising how she was starting to feel about Sarah, she decided now was a good time to reveal to everyone about her secret dates.

She arrived at work and waited for everyone to settle in after the morning meeting. After every morning meeting, they would gather for coffee and gossip about their lives before the day started. The only thing that was different about that particular morning was that Sarah had arrived with coffee for everyone, just as Dante unlocked the front door.

"Good morning, welcome to *Love & Joy*. How can we help you?" welcomed Dante.

"I'm here to introduce myself. I'm...."

"Sarah?" Avery walked in, recognising her voice. She took a deep breath as she turned to make the introductions. "Guys, this is Sarah. We have been dating for the last five months now."

"Well, you kept that quiet," Juliette teased, her eyes wide in surprise.

"Come in, darling, take a seat, tell us all about you," Dante insisted, helping Sarah with the coffees, and leading her over to the sofas.

"I've heard so much about you guys. I feel like I know you already," Sarah smiled, settling in next to Avery.

Dante and Juliette cooed when the couple interlocked fingers.

Sarah and Avery continued to tell them the story of how they met and how each date had gone since. Sarah told them a little about herself. That's when Avery revealed that Milo had known since date one, which made Dante and Juliette fall over laughing. Neither of them knew Milo could keep a secret.

"Wait, are you Sarah Sunny?" Milo gasped as he joined them, pushing Emma in her stroller from her morning walk.

"One and the same."

"Oh wow, Avery. When you said she was an artist, I never knew you meant Sarah Sunny. I've been a huge fan of your work since your first piece with G-A-Art," Milo enthused.

"It's always nice to meet a fan."

"Yeah, Dad took me to New York with him once on one of his business trips, we stumbled upon the gallery by accident, but it was a pretty cool night," Milo said.

"Well, while we are all getting acquainted, Sarah, there is someone I would like you to meet," Avery said, getting up and heading to her daughter.

Scooping Emma up in her arms, the little girl giggled and laughed, smiling at her mother.

"This is the most important person in my life. Emma. My daughter," Avery said.

Emma stretched out her hands towards Sarah, who took the hint and scooped the little child from Avery's arms. Seeing how much Emma responded to Sarah was the sign that Avery needed. It was time for her to tell Sarah the rest of her story. As clients arrived for their meetings,

Sarah wished everyone well, and Avery arranged to meet her for a date at lunch. Sarah agreed, as long as she brought Emma along, which pleased Avery greatly.

❧

At lunch, Avery walked down the street, ecstatic that she had finally introduced Emma to Sarah and that it had gone so well. They decided to meet at Veggie Delight, a new Vegan restaurant that opened only a few weeks prior. Sarah spent most of their date with Emma in her arms. Emma had taken to Sarah as quickly as she had to Milo.

"I'm so happy I finally got to introduce you two," Avery smiled as Emma shook her rattle. "I'm sorry it took so long."

"Don't worry about it. I get it. She's your daughter. You don't want to introduce just anyone to her," Sarah reassured her.

"I.... Sarah.... You know I like you, right? I mean really like you. I might even go as far as saying, I...." Avery struggled with the words and blushed when she couldn't get them out.

"I love you too," Sarah interrupted with a wink laughing as Avery visibly relaxed.

The first time, saying the L-word was always a hard thing to do. After that, it flowed as freely as air.

"Yes, and it's because I love you that I want to tell you something. You have to understand. I have only waited this long because of how others have taken the news in the past. I only reveal this to people who mean a lot to me," Avery began.

"Okay," Sarah said, tucking Emma back into her stroller, giving Avery her undivided attention.

"I am Trans-gender. I was born...."

Sarah stopped her instantly, sensing how scared Avery was anticipating her reaction. Sarah slowly smiled, taking Avery's hands in hers and waiting for Avery to look her in the eyes.

"Can I ask you something?"

Avery nodded nervously.

"Are you happy? The way you are now? Is this the person you want to be?"

"Yes. I feel right. I feel complete. This is me," Avery answered.

"Who we are isn't about our gender; it's who we are in our hearts. I love you, Avery, and as long as you are happy with you, and who you are, then so am I."

"You are truly amazing." Avery smiled, pulling Sarah into her embrace.

Sarah winked. "Well, I try."

Nine

Slowly over the following week, Avery noticed a change in Sarah. Her texts grew less frequent, and when Avery would call, she would make excuses to hurry off the phone. She was either busy with work or had to pop out of town for two days. At first, Avery didn't think anything of it. A big Gallery in L.A. had recently approached Sarah to host their next event. It only made sense that she would throw herself into work. Avery was super happy for her. The exposure would be excellent for her career.

But by the end of the second week, Avery got a twisting feeling in her gut. *Was there more to it*? Avery fretted. Had Sarah accepted Avery's news as easily as she had admitted? Avery didn't want to get in her head too much because she knew she would freak herself out worrying over what was potentially nothing. Instead, she decided to call and see how Sarah was doing.

"Hey baby, how are you? How is work?"

"It's good. Super busy," Sarah replied dryly.

"I can imagine. Do you have any free time over the next week? When is the big event? Need any help?" Avery asked.

"I got it, thanks. Yeah, super busy. I don't know what's going on. I'll get back to you, though. How about we meet for coffee Thursday morning?"

"That sounds great. Well, I will stop distracting you. Enjoy your day. Don't work too hard. I love you,"

"Love you too," Sarah said quickly, ending the call.

With a date set for two days later, Avery relaxed a little. She told herself that she didn't need to worry after all. It was natural to be nervous after revealing a part of yourself to someone new, especially after being vulnerable enough to let someone in your heart and admit that you love them.

On Thursday morning, Avery decided to arrive at *The Golden Coffee Bean* a little early to get coffee and breakfast ready for Sarah to arrive, knowing how busy she was with her art. As the vintage clock on the wall ticked past the hour they were to meet, Avery got that sinking feeling again. She called and texted and received no reply or answer. Deciding to give up, she left Sarah's coffee and croissant on the table and headed to *Love & Joy* with Emma.

Three hours later, Sarah texted apologizing, but Avery was too upset to reply. She wanted to talk about how she was feeling with Dante or Juliette, but with a wedding, a birthday, and a business conference to organize, everyone was too busy to stand around and chat. A part of Avery was glad for the distractions. Keeping herself busy with work stopped her from overthinking and creating scenarios in her head that had her stomach spinning. Still, that didn't stop her from checking her phone constantly throughout the day.

Another week passed, and Avery eventually gave up trying to contact Sarah. Disheartened, she struggled with the feeling of heartbreak. She had revealed the most vulnerable side of herself to Sarah and confessed her love. And since then, she had hardly seen her. She wanted to believe that Sarah wouldn't just up and leave, especially not after Avery told her about how Gemma left. But everything felt all too familiar.

Heading to work one morning, Avery stopped dead in her tracks when she spotted Sarah waiting at their favourite table outside *The Golden Coffee Bean*, two coffees and croissants waiting. Anger roiled through Avery. Her jaw clenched. She couldn't believe Sarah would ignore her attempts to reach out and turn up as though nothing had happened. She decided to ignore Sarah and walk right by.

That didn't work.

"Avery, baby. I'm so happy to see you. Hi, Emma, how are you, sweetheart?" Sarah asked, kneeling to Emma's level and pinching her chubby cheek.

"Are you?" Avery asked, her voice tight.

"Excuse me?"

"Happy to see me? You have been avoiding me for weeks, and now you show up like nothing has happened." Avery felt her anger growing until her hands shook. She was glad to have the handle of the stroller to cling to.

"I know, I'm sorry. I handled all this wrong. Please sit and have coffee. I've missed you."

"I'm late for work, and I don't have time for liars."

"Liars? What the hell, Avery?" Sarah snapped.

"You told me you loved me and then acted the same way Gemma had. You don't do that to someone you love," Avery snarled, pushing past Sarah.

"Avery?.... Avery?" Sarah called after her as Avery rushed off to work, trying to ignore her shaking hands and the tears threatening to fall.

Avery had time to calm down and reflect as she replied to emails, typed up invoices, and checked the accounts. In hindsight, she could have handled things with Sarah differently. She wondered if she'd given up on things forever. She didn't mean to call Sarah a liar. She had let her emotions run away with her. She wished she had given Sarah a chance to explain before snapping. But Avery was a stubborn person and didn't want to be the first to reach out.

Throughout the rest of the day, she held to this resolve. Even as she grew frustrated waiting for a text or call from Sarah, she dug in her heels, telling herself that she would call when she was good and ready.

Ten

MUCH TO AVERY'S SURPRISE, Sarah turned up at *Love & Joy* just before closing. Clients were still in the office. Avery hadn't told anyone about Sarah becoming distant or the argument at the coffee shop that morning. Her heart pounded when she saw the annoyed look creasing Sarah's brow.

"Hi Sarah, are you looking for Avery?" Juliette asked.

"Yeah, is she here?"

Avery stormed from her desk, pulling Sarah to a small corner tucked away from the clients by the front door.

"You turned up at my work? I love these people, but they do not need to see us argue. This is so over the line," Avery whispered angrily.

"Over the line? You called me a liar and then stormed off. I want to talk about this," Sarah replied, drawing herself up to meet her gaze with a hint of defiance and something else Avery couldn't quite define.

"Not here."

"Then were Avery? You stormed off. Let me speak," Sarah pleaded.

"Outside," Avery snapped, storming out the front door, not looking back to see if anyone was watching.

Sarah swiftly followed Avery around the building to the one wall with no windows for clients or co-workers to peek out of.

"Talk," Avery said stiffly, crossing her arms defensively over her chest.

"Me? What about you? I admit I shouldn't have distanced myself. I should have been honest and said I was a little taken back by your news. For that, I will apologize. I'm not an unreasonable person. Are you going to admit you were wrong in calling me a liar?" Sarah snapped.

Avery sighed and relaxed a little. She couldn't argue with Sarah when she had been telling herself all day that she was wrong in how she'd acted.

"I'm sorry for calling you a liar. It's how I felt. You said you love me, that you are fine with who I am, and then you stop texting, answering calls, and stand me up on our date. Like, what the hell? If you're not okay with it, just tell me."

"I'm sorry. After how Gemma left you, I should have handled things better. I struggled for a day or two, adjusting. I've never been with a trans person before, so I didn't know how to take it. I have no issue with you being trans. I stand by what I said that day. As long as you are happy with yourself, then so am I. Please, Avery, I messed up. Can we try again? I've never felt about anyone the way I feel about you. Please don't throw this away," Sarah pleaded, visibly upset.

Avery had never seen that side of Sarah. Seeing her getting upset broke Avery's heart. She didn't want to fight, she also didn't want to lose Sarah, but she didn't think she could take heartbreak again. Avery pulled her into her arms as mascara travelled down Sarah's face.

"I don't want to fight either. Let's draw a line under it. Come to my house tonight for dinner, and we will discuss everything and go from there," Avery said.

"So, are you still my girlfriend?" Sarah asked.

"If you will have me," Avery smiled.

Deciding to approach their relationship with caution, Avery decided to give Sarah a second chance, not just because she loved her but also because of Emma.

Eleven

TWO YEARS later

How time flies when you're having fun. Emma was almost three when Sarah and Avery agreed to try again. It took nearly losing each other to open up a line of communication. After that, Avery and Sarah decided that no matter what, it was better to be honest and risk hurting each other with the truth than hiding things and letting feelings fester to the point someone lost their cool. It turned out for the best because together they became stronger.

After Emma's second birthday, Sarah and Avery decided to look for a place big enough for all of them. It had to be close enough to Sarah's art studio and *Love & Joy*. They were in no rush. They wanted everything to be perfect.

"Hey guys, we have some news," Juliette cheered as Sarah and Avery walked into the office.

"Sit, sit." Dante insisted, struggling to contain his excitement.

"What's up?" Sarah asked, trying to keep up with Emma as she ran around the store.

"We know how busy you both have been trying to find your own place, and with Emma's third birthday approaching, we have decided to take to worry of your hands. Instead, we will plan the perfect teddy bear tea party for her and all her friends from preschool," Juliette said, placing the folder with all the information about the party on the table in front of Avery.

"You guys, this is so beautiful. Thank you." Avery almost couldn't speak around the lump in her throat. She was so overwhelmed by the show of love from her adopted family.

"House hunting is stressful enough, and we love you both so much. We wanted to do something for you," Dante hugged Sarah tightly back.

Sarah and Avery sat Emma down and looked through the folder. Juliette and Dante had thought of everything, and Avery could spot the small touches where even Milo had an input.

The party plan was so sweet. It was organized for the park with a huge gazebo. There would be a large round table decorated with a baby pink and white tablecloth, and matching chair covers. The table was decorated with multiple little tea sets, and next to each chair was a smaller one for each child's favourite Teddy bear. In addition, each child would have their own calligraphy place setting and a personalised goodie bag as a keepsake for the day.

After the tea party, there was going to be a cake styled like a teddy bear made up of a large multi-tiered bear-shaped cake and cupcakes. Entertainment would include a magic show, puppet show, and a petting zoo with a Disney princess-themed disco to end the day.

"This is so beautiful," Sarah said, her voice catching at the level of detail and thought put into the event. "You guys are so awesome."

"Well, Avery and Emma are family, and when you and Avery got together, you joined our family. So now, I will take Emma to preschool, and you two have an appointment with the realtor over on Summershore strip, by the lake," Milo grinned, struggling to hide the secret he was obviously keeping.

"We didn't have any viewings today," Avery said, confused, eyeing her friends with suspicion.

"Oh yes, you do. We called in a favour. Choosing a home is deeply personal, but I couldn't help myself when I saw this. You have to see it. It would be perfect for you," Dante cheered, clapping his hands in excitement.

Avery and Sarah accepted Dante's help even if they thought he may have been a touch too involved. On the drive to the address he gave them, they discussed how to thank him but politely ask him to leave them to find their home on their own.

All issues went out the window, vanishing on the breeze when they pulled up to the house tucked into the hillside. White picket fences surrounded a small garden. The porch was twice the size of Avery's, with enough space for a porch swing and dining set to enjoy breakfast in the garden. Three storeys showed off a mix of modern and gothic architecture. It was stunning.

As the realtor walked them from room to room, they fell in love with the house. The kitchen with its central island was bigger than the entire first floor of Avery's current home and opened up into a large living and dining area. A spiral staircase led to the next floor, which consisted of two bedrooms. The master had its own en suite bathroom, and the second bedroom was perfect for Emma, right next to the family bathroom. The best part was the attic, a massive space with skylight windows that framed the sky beautifully.

"Dante said this would be perfect for a private art studio," the realtor said.

Sarah turned to Avery with tears in her eyes. Avery's skin tingled with goosebumps. The house was perfect. It was everything they could have dreamed of and more.

At Emma's teddy bear tea party, while the children played, danced, and enjoyed watching their parents attempt to make balloon animals, Sarah and Avery decided to share their good news with the group.

"You put an offer in on the house?" Dante cheered with tears of joy in his eyes.

"We did, and even better, they accepted it! We move in next week," Avery answered.

"Darlings, that's amazing. I'm so happy for you," Juliette cheered, flinging her arms tightly around them both.

Looking at the joy in her daughter's eyes and the way she laughed and played with her friends, Avery was struck with a sense of gratitude. Summershore had been the best thing for her. Emma was thriving. Watching as the little girl ran excitedly over to Sarah with her blue balloon-shaped poodle, Avery was close to tears. Seeing Sarah with Emma and knowing that soon they would all be sharing a home, Avery realised it was the happiest she had ever been. Life was good and beautiful, and she couldn't want anything else.

After the tea party, Sarah carried a very tired Emma in her arms and wished everyone well, not forgetting to thank everyone for their help and kindness. Avery gave Dante, Juliette, and Milo thank you gifts. Milo received the latest video game that Avery knew he had been saving up for, and Dante was given front row tickets to the latest concert at the orchestra hall. Juliette was given a selection of things for her upcoming honeymoon with Damian. Juliette had married Damian the previous year, but with wedding season keeping everyone at *Love & Joy* busy, they had been forced to delay their honeymoon until things weren't quite so busy.

Twelve

MOVING into their new home was stressful, but Avery and Sarah welcomed the challenge with open arms. Saving each hectic night in their memories, looking at them as the first seeds in the garden that was their love.

"Diamonds are forged under pressure. All this stress is the pressure needed to make our life shine," Sarah said.

Avery laughed and kissed her. "You are so poetic sometimes."

Emma loved her bedroom, which Sarah had decorated herself. The wall behind her bed had a jungle mural painted over it with some of Emma's favourite animal cartoon characters. Avery turned out to be a dab hand with carpentry and DIY, building Emma a small stage area in the corner of her room for whenever she wanted to perform to her teddy bear audience. Avery had recently started Emma in ballet and found that she loved it, taking to it like a duck to water. The girl was a natural.

Having the loft space, Sarah sold her old studio, putting the money towards saving for the future. Together, they moved all her art supplies to the attic. Avery would spend many nights cooking beautiful dinners in the kitchen and dancing around the living room. Their little home was everything they had dreamed of and more.

"Welcome back, Mrs. .... wow, look at that tan. The Bahamas looks good on you," Avery cheered, welcoming Juliette back to *Love & Joy*.

"How was the honeymoon?" Dante asked.

"Wonderful, I almost didn't want to come back. But I couldn't leave you guys. I missed you!" Juliette sighed, smiling like a love-struck teenager.

"So come on then, now the fun part," Avery smiled.

"Fun part?" Juliette asked, confused.

"Yeah, for us. Pictures, woman, we need to see pictures," Dante cheered, placing a tray full of freshly made coffee and breakfast pastries on the table.

"Where was it you stayed again?" Dante asked, tucking into some grapes.

"Cape Santa Maria, we had our own private villa right on the beach." Juliette handed him photographs of the view from their room.

White sand beaches, sunsets over the sea. The pictures looked like heaven, but Avery's favourite photos were not of the beautiful land-scapes or the sunsetting of an evening. It was the pictures of Damian and Juliette together, sharing their evening meal wrapped in each other's arms. Staring lovingly into each other's eyes and laughing.

"They say a picture speaks a thousand words; these pictures screamed a dictionary. Just so much love and beauty. What you and Damian have...it's like movie love." Avery cooed, unable to take her eyes off the images.

Juliette smiled back. "You are too sweet. I always thought that's what you and Sarah had."

Movie love, Avery thought. Every time she thought of Sarah, her heart skipped a beat. Every time she looked at her smile, her stomach filled with butterflies. Every bit of good news, every bit of bad, she wanted to share it all with Sarah. Sarah had quickly become the centre of Avery's world.

Movie love. She couldn't get the words out of her head all day. As she locked up to head home, Avery stopped, staring at the beautiful sign above the front door. *Love & Joy* was the perfect name. In its simplicity, it spoke to everything she felt about Sarah. That was when she knew what she had to do.

With Emma in bed and Avery finishing up her latest art piece upstairs, Avery took out her laptop and searched online for the perfect ring. She wanted something different because Sarah wasn't just any woman. She had a unique sense of style, one which changed day to day solely based on her mood. Avery wanted something that represented the love she felt filling her heart and the beauty Sarah had brought to her life.

Keeping a close eye on the stairs, not wanting Sarah to see what she was searching for, Avery scrolled countless websites, but nothing spoke to her. Solitaires were too obvious, and princess cuts too simple. Halo rings seemed too blingy for Sarah, but then she saw it. A yellow gold band with a black emerald cut diamond, more petite with pale pink pear-shaped sapphires on either side, and diamonds cascading down the shoulders. It was perfect and spoke to the ups and downs, the light and dark moments of their relationship. It was perfect. She clicked the reserve button and arranged a viewing of the ring the following day. She didn't want to wait. She knew that ring was *the ring* and couldn't wait to see Sarah's face.

As soon as Avery held the ring in her hand, she knew no other ring would capture how she felt about Sarah. She didn't bother to try and haggle the way she had heard so many of her clients had. Slapping down her credit card, she bought the ring on the spot.

"Your girlfriend is going to love this. How do you plan on proposing?" asked the clerk.

Avery had given it a lot of thought. Smiling back, she answered, "I'm planning a scavenger hunt. I will start by leaving her a note on her pillow to take her to the place we first met. I will ask my friend Frank who fixed her car, to hand her the next clue. Each clue will lead to another significant spot in our relationship. She'd finally end up back at home. I will have a candlelit dinner prepared, rose petals, champagne, the works."

"That is so beautiful. Congratulations."

Thirteen

AVERY WANTED the proposal to be perfect. While she felt the ring burning a hole in her pocket and wanted to scream her love for Sarah from the rooftops, she kept herself in check. She wanted their proposal story to be one that their family would talk about for years.

Every detail had to be perfect. One evening, she typed up a list of all the moments she wanted to capture in her proposal. Starting with the day they met, their first date, and *Straws & Umbrellas*, to when Sarah gave Avery her painting. She wanted the scavenger hunt to be a journey through time and showcase everything they had been through together, both the highs and the lows. She even picked the location of their first big fight, as well as the second and third, she also wanted Emma to be involved somehow because Emma meant so much to them both.

Hours later, she had her memory roadmap and began her spreadsheet of clues for each one. With each completed clue, her excitement grew. With Sarah's birthday approaching, Avery decided that would be the day she asked Sarah to be her wife. She could disguise the proposal as a birthday treat, telling her she would be hunting for presents.

Wow, I never knew I was so romantic. Avery smiled.

"What shall we do for your birthday?" Avery asked, knowing full well what she already had planned.

"I don't want to do anything. It's fine. It's not a big birthday anyway. You know us women, never wanting to admit being a year older," Sarah joked.

"Don't be silly. It's a celebration," Avery insisted.

"I said I don't want to do anything, okay? Just drop it. Besides, I'm super busy with work right now," Sarah snapped.

Avery was taken aback by Sarah's reaction. It had been a simple question, and she hadn't even fought too hard against her response. What was up with her? Avery was worried Sarah was under too much stress with work. She knew she was planning on opening her gallery. Perhaps she had taken on more than she could handle. Avery and Sarah had always been open with each other, sharing their burdens, so when Sarah became distant and distracted, Avery began to worry.

She didn't want to pry in case she pushed Sarah away, deciding instead to allow her space. It was hard to accept that she would come to her when she was ready to talk when all Avery wanted to do was shake her and beg her to tell her what was wrong.

Sarah's birthday approached. It was only two days before the big day. The more Sarah pulled away, the more Avery questioned if proposing was the right thing to do. One evening, staring at the ceiling, unable to sleep, Avery's mind flashed to the yellow envelope, the divorce papers, and the pain she'd felt when she came home to find Gemma gone. It didn't hurt anymore thinking of Gemma but imagining the same scenario with Sarah terrified Avery. Losing Sarah meant a heartbreak Avery didn't think she could survive. *I can't carry on like this. I'm going to talk to her in the morning,* she told herself before forcing her eyes shut and going to sleep.

The following morning Avery woke up in bed alone. A note on the bedside table read:

'Got a meeting in LA. I've taken Emma to preschool. See you at dinner.
S xxx'

Avery sat in her car outside *Love & Joy* for fifteen minutes, staring blankly into space. She was full of energy but was not motivated to do anything. The thought of life without Sarah felt empty. Slowly she felt her mind spiralling.

Stop it. Nothing has happened. You just bought a house together. Pull yourself together!

Avery dragged herself from her car. She tried to repeat her pep talk in her head but found the once comforting words did little to motivate her. Pushing the office door open, Avery jumped back, almost tripping, and screamed as party poppers and confetti cannons exploded around her.

"Surprise!" cheered everyone in the room.

"What the hell? You almost gave me a heart attack!" Avery gasped, clutching her hand to her chest, making everyone laugh.

After a few moments and her nerves settled, Avery's mouth fell open. The room was filled with white and pink roses. Canvases filled the walls, all painted by Sarah. Each canvas depicted different stages in their relationship. Their first date. When Sarah met Emma. Buying their first home. In the middle of the room, Sarah was on one knee under a golden balloon arch. It wasn't until Avery looked at the balloon arch again that she saw the balloons spelled out, 'Will you marry me?'

"What?.....what?....." Avery stuttered, utterly lost for words.

"Avery, you have been a light in my life I didn't know I needed until I found you. You encourage me, bring out the best in me and inspire me. You didn't just invite me into your life. You invited me into your family. This family," Sarah began, tears causing her eyes to sparkle like stars.

Juliette, Dante, Damian, Milo, and Emma huddled together, watching and waiting in anticipation.

"You are the most beautiful woman I have ever met, both inside and out. You have so much love to give. You share it with your clients every day, you share it with your family and friends, and you opened your heart and home to a child who needed it most. Words will never be enough to describe how I truly feel about you. But I hope this ring will, so, Avery Lannister.... Will you marry me?" Sarah asked, her voice cracking as the question left her lips.

Avery felt like she might pass out. Her head spun; her hands shook. Overwhelmed by the love that filled the room, the heartfelt words from Sarah, and the loving gaze from Emma as she clung to Sarah as if she, too, waited for Avery's reply. Avery realised that Sarah hadn't been pulling away after all. She hadn't been cold and distant. It had all been in her head. It was too much. Avery burst out crying and laughing at the same time.

Confusion filled the faces of everyone. Was her reaction good? Bad? No one wanted to ask.

"Yes, I will marry you.... on one condition...." Avery began as she reached into her purse, pulling out the ring and presenting it to Sarah. "If you will marry me too."

"Oh my god, this is too beautiful," Dante chirped, wiping tears from his eyes.

Sarah's smile lit up the room. "Of course, I will!"

Placing their engagement rings on each other's fingers Avery and Sarah pulled each other into a hug, sealing their betrothal with a kiss.

"Congratulations!" Everyone cheered.

"Ha! This is defiantly new; I've never seen a couple where both parties have an engagement ring before," Milo joked.

Fourteen

JULIETTE AND DANTE took over wedding planning just like they had with Emma's birthday party, but the brides insisted on having some input this time. They both had so many ideas, but one thing was for sure: They wanted a wedding that represented them both equally. After months of planning, too many ideas, and a few disagreements with Dante, it was settled.

They would have an outdoor wedding at the lake house. The ceremony would take place under the big blossoming oak tree with chandeliers holding small battery-operated tea lights - for safety, of course – would hang from white and black sheets of fabric draped over the larger branches. Both brides would have matching bouquets of black cilia lilies and pink roses. The reception would be decorated in a rustic theme with subtle hints of Sarah's graffiti art and rock-chick style. The centrepieces on each table would be candles framing vintage vinyl records, each one having a different song that held meaning for the happy couple. Milo thought it would be adorable to have Emma wear a pink ballerina style dress with a little leather jacket with 'I love my mommies' written across the back.

Music would be a string quartet for the ceremony and a harpist during the meal. Sarah insisted her brother's punk rock band perform a few songs later in the evening at the reception. When they were not performing, there would be a DJ. It was going to be a wedding of beauty, love, music, and art; a true representation of Avery and Sarah. One thing that Avery and Sarah insisted on was keeping their wedding outfits hidden from each other. That was the one thing they each wanted to be a surprise.

"Oh my.... this is it.... this is the dress," Avery said from behind the changing room door.

"Come on, then let me see." Juliette cheered.

Avery stepped out of the changing room in a floor-length figure-hugging modern glamour mermaid dress. Illusion lace travelled from the spaghetti straps down the plunging V-neck neckline and flowed along the bodice to the waist. The skirt trailed behind and offered a pink dip-dye effect. Avery looked magical, like a princess, bringing Juliette to tears.

"Avery.... wow, you look..."

"Bootiful mommy," Emma said, clapping her hands and jumping up and down on Juliette's knee.

Standing at the altar, Avery stood filled with nerves and excitement. Juliette was honoured when Avery asked her to be her maid of honour, and she stood by her side with pride, holding her hand. The music started, and the guests fell silent. Avery turned slowly to see Sarah, her arm linked with her dad's, gliding towards her. Emma held tight to Sarah's other hand. Sarah looked a vision in her floor-length black V-neck long-sleeved gown. The gold flowers and vine detail covering every inch gave Sarah a glamorous look. She reminded Avery of a movie star walking the red carpet.

"Do you Avery Lannister?"

"I do."

"Do you, Sarah...."

"I do!" Sarah jumped in too excited to let the officiant finish her name.

"It gives me great pleasure to pronounce you married."

The day flew by in a blur. Avery couldn't take her eyes off Sarah. The ceremony was simple, beautiful, and didn't leave a dry eye in the house. Everyone celebrated with cocktails, music, dancing, and Sarah's surprise graffiti show. At the reception, she painted a picture of the moment they'd said, "I do."

It was a wedding like no other. A wedding true to two people who were meant to be together. True love. True family. True, love and joy.

⌒

"Dante, I can't thank you and Juliette enough for organizing all this. It's magnificent." Avery smiled.

"It was an honour, my dear," Dante replied, clinking his glass in cheers.

"I haven't seen you on the dance floor."

"Ha! You won't, not will all these loved-up songs. Who would I dance with?" Dante asked.

"I did notice David isn't here. Is everything okay?"

"It's your wedding, don't you worry about me," Dante grinned, obviously trying to mask his hurt.

"Dante?"

"Alright, fine.... we split up. We are staying friends; it just wasn't meant to be. But don't you worry that beautiful face. I really am fine," Dante said, squeezing Avery's face between his palms and making her laugh.

"Love will find you one day, and I will have the honour of organizing your wedding. I promise," Avery said, hugging him tightly.

"I'm sure you will," Dante said, patting her softly on the back.

His words may have been said in agreement, but Avery was no fool. She could tell Dante was hurting and hiding it well. But she didn't want to upset him. He was a strong guy, and he knew when and if he wanted to talk, she would be there for him.

"Come, dance with me on my wedding day." Avery smiled, leading Dante to the dance floor.

Fifteen

VERONA. The home of Shakespeare's star-crossed lovers Romeo and Juliette. A place steeped in medieval architecture, rich history, art, and everything needed to celebrate Avery and Sarah's first anniversary. Juliette and Damian had kindly volunteered to look after Emma for the week, allowing the head-over-heels in love couple a much-needed break just the two of them.

When they were not enjoying the beautiful open-air markets, soaking up the beautiful city's history, and taking tours, Avery and Sarah enjoyed a new restaurant and cafe every day. They wanted to sample everything and go home with fabulous stories to tell all their friends. Sarah had taken multiple pictures for inspiration for her art when she got home, and Avery had collected a small number of souvenirs as tokens from their trip.

The year since they married had flown by so quickly, but Avery had loved every second. Sarah gasped for breath as Avery laughed. Sarah had wanted to take the elevator, but Avery had insisted on the stairs, saying they both needed the exercise after all the food they had been indulging in since they arrived. Their trip was due to end the following day, and Avery wanted to soak up as much of Italy as she could before they left.

The view over Verona from the top of the tower at Torre Dei

Lamberti was breath-taking. Buildings for as far as the eye could see, sights you could miss just walking the streets. It was a wonderful place to take a step back, breathe, and reflect.

A house. A home. A family. Avery had everything she had ever wanted. The previous year had been crazy but in the best possible way. They had moved into their home, got married, and Sarah had finally accomplished her dream of opening her own art gallery. Avery's career with *Love & Joy* had gone from strength to strength, with Juliette finally agreeing to look at opening a second store out of town. Emma was thriving and loved Sarah so much that it made Avery's heart want to burst with joy. Separately, Avery and Sarah were doing great. Together, they were an unstoppable team, and as a family, they were unbreakable.

They say that the honeymoon period fades just as quickly as it starts. But as Avery turned to look at Sarah, she realised that the old saying was a lie. Their love, spark, and flame were an inferno with no sign of burning out any time soon.

"I can't believe we are here," Avery breathed.

"What? We have been here a week," Sarah teased.

"No, silly. I mean here. Us, together. A family."

Sarah wrapped her arms around Avery's waist, hugging her tightly to her chest and resting her chin on Avery's shoulder. Snuggled tightly in her wife's embrace, the pair stood silently staring out over the beauty that was Verona, Italy. Content with just enjoying each other, the sights, the smells, and the sound of life bustling below their feet.

Reflecting was beautiful, but Avery couldn't wait to see what else the future had in store.

"I was thinking.... how would you feel about adding to our little family?" Sarah whispered in Avery's ear.

"Like a puppy?" Avery asked, her heart beating a little faster despite the playful tone.

"No....like adopting another child. Maybe a little boy," Sarah ventured.

Avery spun around to face Sarah, her skin igniting in goosebumps. Her heart felt like it was growing ten times as fast, filled to bursting.

"Are you serious?" Avery asked, trying to control the smile that stretched ear to ear.

"I've been thinking about it for a while. What do you think?"

"I love it! Let's do it!" Avery cheered.

On the plane home, watching Italy slip away and confirming their anniversary celebration was coming to an end, Avery half expected to feel the usual holiday blues. But with the prospect of adding to their family, she couldn't wait to get home. She missed Emma dearly. They both did. But she also couldn't wait to see the look on Emma's face when she found out she would be a sister.

"Hey guys, how was Verona?!" Damian asked, welcoming them both inside.

"Wonderful, we couldn't have picked a better place. I have so many ideas for the gallery. I can't wait to get back to the studio," Sarah replied.

"Mommies," came Emma's sweet voice running from the living room, closely followed by Juliette and Milo.

Avery knelt and wrapped Emma in the biggest hug she could.

"I missed you," Emma said.

"We missed you too, sweetie, but we have a surprise for you," Avery said, looking to Sarah for confirmation.

"A surprise, what is it? What is it?" Cheered Emma bouncing up and down in excitement.

"How would you feel about having a little brother?" Sarah asked, kneeling to join her family.

Emma shrieked out her excitement, wrapping her tiny arms as far around Avery and Sarah as she could before running around Juliette's hallway, cheering to everyone who would listen.

"Milo! Milo! I'm going to have a baby brother. I get to be a big sister," Emma cheered, jumping up at Milo.

"You will make an amazing big sister Emma!" Milo smiled.

"You guys are just too perfect." Juliette smiled, wiping away a tear as she smiled back at Avery.

"Congratulations, guys!" Damian grinned.

"Well, we only decided on the way home, but we will do it, and we can't wait," Sarah confirmed.

"Seeing the love you two have for each other and how wonderful you both are with Emma, it will not be long before you hold your little boy in your arms," Milo said.

"Have you told Dante yet?" asked Milo.

"No, why don't we call him now? Avery grinned, pulling out her phone and hitting the video call button.

It didn't take long for Dante to answer and even less time before he screamed so loud Emma had to cover her ears, and everyone erupted into laughter.

"Mommy, Sarah?" Emma asked, tugging on Sarah's jacket.

"Yes, sugar plum?"

"While I wait for my baby brother, can I get a kitten?" Emma asked sweetly, peering up with the biggest and cutest eyes she could muster.

"Ha, ha. What do you think, Avery?" Sarah asked.

"Sure, sweetie, we'll go to the shelter this weekend," Avery answered.

"Yay! I get a baby brother and a kitten! You are the best. I love my mommies!"

A house, a home, and an ever-growing family. Avery had everything she ever wanted, and it felt better than she ever could have imagined.

Without realising she was even looking for it, she had found home.

The End

Something Blue

THE WEDDING TRIO BOOK 3

One

DANTE SAT and watched Sarah and Avery dancing together. The night was almost over, but the atmosphere was still electric. A tear brimmed his eyes, and his heart grew warm, sharing in their love for one another. The look on their faces when they saw the venue all decorated for the first time, the nuances and little details that spoke to them. It meant so much. It was a day they would never forget.

Dante was a hopeless romantic; he loved love. And being a part of a couple's special day meant he could experience new love all the time. Organising a wedding meant structure, organisation, lists, and everything Dante enjoyed to the fullest. All the things that helped him calm his mind and distract him from the shitty parts of the world.

Dante had been in love before. Several times actually. But he had yet to walk down the aisle himself. He was content in being a part of other people's big day, but he never fancied that day for himself. He never told anyone about how he felt. How could he explain that he loved love but never wanted to get married? What would his clients think if he told them that he believed it unnecessary and doomed to fail? It was ironic considering how much he loved planning weddings.

Dante loved hearing others' love stories and what brought them together, each such a different, exciting tale, pulling at the heartstrings and sparking hope. A hope that Dante would always ignore. Instead, he chose to live his life enjoying love without the pressures of finding *the one*. He looked at a wedding as a puzzle; he tasked himself with finding all the missing pieces to make the happy couple smile and bask in the result.

Weddings were beautiful, a time to bring people together, a time to share love and forget about everything else. It was the togetherness, the love that every person in the room shared that Dante loved; spreading happiness and joy was so important. In a world already so full of conflict and heartache, a wedding was the one time that all differences were put aside. And instead of tearing each other down, people wished the best for each other.

When he found the job at *Love and Joy*, it was a dream come true. A chance to enjoy that excitement and joy every day, a chance to immerse himself into organising and planning – his favourite things! And when Juliette had offered him ownership over part of the business after he helped it expand, he was over the moon. Something that was his that he could nurture and grow and help bring that feeling to others. It was his own. It was his calling.

Wedding and parties always made him feel special, like he was in the cool kid club. They made him feel light as air, like he might take off flying at a moment's notice. His footsteps would be lighter, and every day he would look forward to checking off a new task on his list; watching the seeds he had planted flourish into beautiful flowers. Every night he would go to bed with a sense of accomplishment and satisfaction. No other job he had worked before gave him that feeling.

Every cloud has a silver lining. But in Dante's experience, every sunny day had a cloud. It was that little voice of doubt in Dante's mind that made him wonder how long a marriage would last. He would watch the couples on their big day with hope and prayer that they would be back to plan an anniversary or celebrate the birth of a child in a few years. He hated it when he could tell a couple was getting married because they felt obligated to after being together for so long or because of family ties—those weddings were doomed to fail and reinforced the fact that Dante would never get married.

Dante helped plan every wedding that came through *Love and Joy*, and that little voice would ask him, *Have you done enough? Will this wedding be enough?* A small part of him wanted to believe that if the wedding was perfect, if the couple was so overwhelmed with joy and memories to remind them of why they chose to get married, then maybe, just maybe, that marriage would be a success.

Two

DANTE FIRST FELL in love with weddings when he was ten; when his mother and father were getting married. His parents saved their money for years to afford their wedding. And the time had finally arrived. Dante loved seeing his mother so happy, finalising all of the details, picking out a colour scheme, and smiling as she crossed off the days on the calendar.

When the day finally came, everything was beautiful. And seeing his mother and father staring at each other with nothing but love in their eyes was perfect. As Dante grew up, he would pull out their photo album and stare at the pictures, remembering all the feelings from that day.

A couple of years later, when the arguments started and his parents spent less time together, Dante relied on that little photo album more often. Memories of a happier time. His parents didn't notice it was missing, so Dante kept it hidden under his bed for safekeeping.

One night, when he woke to hear his mother crying in the kitchen, he snuck out of bed carrying the photo album in hopes of cheering her up; his heart broke when it didn't work. The following day, he woke up to find his father was gone. He never saw him again.

It was only years later that his memory of what happened that night came back. He assumed he had blocked out the memory or dreamt it. But he hadn't.

"You trapped me! I never wanted kids; I never wanted to get married. I did all that because I cared. And look what it's gotten me. I don't know who I am anymore, and that's because of *you*. Goodbye, Keira!" His father had screamed.

The years went by and Dante watched his mother try to replicate the love she had for his father. First came Darius, a doctor from Chicago. That marriage failed when he cheated. Next came Tom, the car salesman. That marriage ended because Tom worked too much, and Keira didn't like the lack of attention. The third was Jerry. He said that Keira was too needy. Each time, Keira had seemed happy and the wedding was beautiful. But the marriage never lasted. As Dante grew older and helped his mother while she cried, saying how she thought this one was the one, Dante realised that marriage wasn't something he ever wanted.

He loved weddings, love, and the beauty of romance. But the thought of feeling that love and comfort, only to sit there in heartbreak when it all fell apart was too much. Watching his mother search for 'the one,' and spending so much of her life searching for what she thought was the answer to all her problems only to be disappointed, he could not bear it. It was draining, and Dante didn't want to live his life like that.

With each marriage, Dante watched Keira change. She would lose a part of herself, and vice versa, her partner did as well. From what Dante knew of love, it was meant to be good and pure. It was a partnership, each person bringing out the best in the other. A partnership based on love and support, and being each other's strengths not weaknesses. What he saw of love from his mother's list of failed marriages was not love. When he got the job at Love and Joy, Keira had asked her son to plan her upcoming wedding. It had been the first wedding that Dante had refused to plan. He wanted no part in it.

Three

"GOOD MORNING," Dante cheered as he arrived at work.

"Someone seems extra chipper this morning," Juliette grinned.

"I'm still basking in the glory of Avery and Sarah's wedding last night," Dante sighed, settling in behind his desk with his coffee.

"It was a beautiful night. You should be proud, some of your best work yet," Juliette said, raising her mug in cheers.

"Oh please, it was a team effort. I wonder what our happy couple is up to this morning."

"Probably getting ready for their honeymoon."

Dante sighed, looking at the spot on the wall where they planned to hang the picture of Avery and Sarah's wedding day.

"I love this feeling. The day after, you know, when it's gone well. It's one of my favourite parts of this job," Dante said.

"I know exactly what you mean. We can't relax for too long. We still have plenty of other people waiting for us to make their event special," Juliette got up and stretched.

"Just a little longer," Dante chuckled, swinging back and forth in his chair.

With Avery scheduled to be off work for the next three weeks for her honeymoon, Dante and Juliette were working double time. They had planned to make more time to manage the workload, but it didn't leave much time to sit and relax. Thankfully, working through to-do lists and finding solutions to tricky situations was where Dante thrived.

When a florist had double booked for a sweet sixteenth and had to cancel, Dante found a new supplier last minute with the same floral arrangement for half the price. When save the dates arrived with the wrong names, Dante fixed it, all while making sure he and Juliette were full of coffee and well-fed.

"You are superhuman," Juliette yawned at the end of the day. "How are you still so full of energy? I'm beat."

"This is what I live for, darling, have a good night; I will see you in the morning," Dante kissed Juliette on the forehead, leaving her to lock up before heading home.

Dante woke the following morning to several texts from Juliette. There was an issue with one of the brides of a wedding they were planning. Claudia had gained a reputation from the second she walked into Love and Joy as being a bridezilla. Every detail had to be run by her and triple-checked before it was signed off on. She would call at all hours of the night and make changes once details had already been confirmed. Her wedding was fast approaching. But since everything took three times as long, Juliette was concerned that they would not have the wedding prepared on time, if the bride-to-be carried on at the rate she was going. It would be the first time Love and Joy failed to pull off an event if that happened.

"Hey, Juliette, what's up?" Dante asked as he rushed to get ready.

"It's Claudia Herman; she has had me up all night," Juliette yawned back through the phone.

"Oh dear, what is the problem this time?"

"Catering. One of her friends debunked the cater we had already chosen, something about not having enough of a following on social media. Apparently, this bride insists on only having vendors with huge followings."

"How can I help?"

"I need to get at least a few more hours sleep, and I have meetings all day, and then I have to set up the medical conference out of town. Can you contact her chosen caterer and set us a last-minute tasting?"

"Sure, email me over the details," Dante agreed, jumping in his car.

When Dante arrived at Love and joy, he sent out a few emails rearranging his appointments for the day and updated his schedule. He was determined this bridezilla would not mess up the other events he was organising. Finally, he checked the email from Juliette, and he sighed deeply in frustration. The caterer Claudia had chosen was Ben Ramos.

Dante had worked with Ben on several events before and was not looking forward to working with him again, especially on bridezilla's wedding. Ben had a reputation as being difficult to work with. And the few times Ben and Dante worked together, Ben had run late and valued his own opinion over the customers. Dante thought Ben had an inflated ego and hated the way he barked orders at everyone like they worked for him – Dante included.

"Juliette, seriously? Ben Ramos? We couldn't have found anyone else to work with on this wedding?" Dante complained as Juliette arrived.

Juliette was still sleepy and stressed; her hair was messy, and she had coffee down her blouse, yawning and brewing a fresh pot. She stretched out her shoulders and ran a frustrated hand over her face.

"I know, believe me, but she asked specifically for him. I have so much to do today, and I've spilt coffee all over myself, trying to avoid a learner driver on my way in. Can you please, *please*, deal with it for me? I don't think I have the energy for it today," Juliette yawned.

"Of course, I will. I just hope he doesn't make things harder for us."

"Me too," Juliette smiled, heading to her office to change her shirt.

Dante called Ben but only reached his voicemail. Checking his social media, Dante realised he had been out partying the night before and was most likely sleeping off a hangover. Rolling his eyes, he picked up his phone and tried the next best thing. Calling Claudia.

"Hi, Claudia. It's Dante from Love and Joy. I'm having difficulty reaching Mr. Ramos; however, I have several other caterers who offer similar menus to his. Would you like me to set up a tasting with one of those?" Dante asked as sweetly as he could summon.

"No! I specifically asked for Ben Ramos. I don't want anyone else. I'm paying you a lot of money for this wedding. How hard is it to do a simple tasting? I have so many things I need to do today. Do I need to do your job for you too?" Claudia snapped into the phone.

"Of course not; I am aware of your busy schedule and was simply hoping to offer you an alternative to work with."

"Thank you for your consideration," Claudia began, her gentle tone was a shock compared to every other interaction Dante had with her so far. "But as I said, I'm paying for a service, so get me Ben Ramos, and I need the tasting by three this afternoon. Got it?" Claudia snapped, slamming the phone down.

"Well, she's a treat," Dante muttered with a huge sigh. He took a big sip of his cappuccino, rearranged the buttons on his blazer, and mustered his inner wedding planner to continue his day.

After several more attempts, Dante finally managed to get hold of Ben's assistant and arranged the last-minute tasting, but on the grounds of a five per cent increase on his usual fee.

"Of course, he is always thinking of the money. Materialistic, childish fool," Dante mumbled.

He carried on with his day and got through as much work as he could before rushing off to the Fisher Hotel for the tasting. Dante didn't know what he was dreading more: working with Ben or bearing witness to Claudia's reaction when Ben did what Ben did best – put himself first.

Four

To Dante's surprise, Ben's team had arrived on time and was already setting up for the tasting. A printed-off menu of potential dishes lay on the tables, ready for when Miss Herman arrived. Servers were on standby, and a team of bar staff stood with bottles of wine that complimented each dish. Dante was impressed. *Perhaps Ben had turned over a new leaf. Maybe I was too quick to judge.*

But Dante was rarely wrong about anyone, and he took his job very seriously. Heading into the kitchen, he found Lucy – Ben's sous chef – but no Ben. Searching the rest of the area and the car park, he realised Ben's car wasn't there. *Typical. Late again*, Dante huffed.

As three o'clock approached, Dante began to panic. Claudia was on her way, and from the last communication Dante had with her, she was bringing two of her friends, one of whom was a known social media influencer with a vicious tongue when it came to reviews. Dante tried to call Ben again, but his call went to voicemail. Running into the kitchen, Dante looked around to see Ben's team had made a start on some of the dishes, but the main courses hadn't been touched, and they were time-consuming dishes.

"Lucy! The lamb and the salmon dishes, tell me you know how to make them." Dante pleaded, sliding out the way as chefs moved from stovetop to stovetop.

"Yeah, but Ben will not like it if I start them without him; plus, I don't have his seasoning list. He keeps them very secret. No one knows them," Lucy hurriedly answered.

"I don't care. There is no sign of him, and I can't reach him on the phone. You will just have to start without him. Miss Herman is on her way, and I will only be able to stall her for so long. We cannot afford to piss her off."

"He won't like it."

"Right now, I don't give a hoot what Ben Ramos likes. If he wanted things done his way, he should have arrived here on time," Dante snapped and turned on his heels to stall for as long as he could.

Heading back outside to try and call Ben once more, Dante watched as Claudia arrived with her friends. All three of them were dressed in almost identical all-white outfits with their Chanel purses, stiletto heels, and oversized sunglasses.

"Good afternoon, Miss Herman. You look stunning," Dante welcomed her with a light kiss on both cheeks.

"I know. I see Ben Ramos is here. I'm glad we got all that mess sorted out. Now, let's move on with this tasting; I have a lot to do," Claudia snapped her fingers, brushing past Dante and heading to the private dining room.

Dante followed close behind and helped Claudia and her friends settle in, making small talk about the wedding, hoping to stall the women long enough for Ben to arrive. But flattery and getting the women to boast and brag about themselves could only last for so long, especially with Claudia being known for having little to no patience.

"Ok, I think I have kept you gabbing for long enough. Let's get this tasting underway," Dante smiled, heading to the kitchen to check on the appetizers.

Dante panicked when he realised that Ben still had not arrived. And Lucy was no closer to having the tasters for the main courses finished. Dante was not one to panic for long. He knew little about Ben's menu but enough to ramble on about it long enough for Lucy to finish the dishes. He swooned and encouraged the ladies to enjoy their tasting, bringing them fresh summery cocktails in oversized glasses. He put on his best girlfriend bestie attitude and convinced them to picture and post the tasting on social media as it was happening.

"This *live* action capturing of your taste testing will surely attract more followers." Dante clasped his hands together and shamelessly made use of his sexy voice. Though he wished it had the same effect on male prospects, he knew straight women lapped it up.

The appetizers were a huge success, and after a lot of discussion, Claudia picked the one she wanted for her wedding. Dante tried to stall a bit longer by asking the bar staff about the wine sections.

"What about the main course?" Samantha asked, checking her watch, and becoming impatient, her mood instantly rubbing off on Claudia.

"The main courses will just be a little while longer. You know Mr. Ramos. He is a perfectionist," Dante reassured. "How about while we wait, we try out more cocktails?"

"I didn't order cocktails," Claudia said.

"No, you didn't, but as you are a special client of Love and Joy, we are offering you a complimentary cocktail hour with personalized drinks for your special day," Dante smiled.

"That sounds great. No one else will have anything like it. Cocktails that are all about *you*, it's *perfect*," enthused Natalie, Claudia's other friend.

Dante convinced the bar staff to create a list of unique, on-the-spot cocktails. And to his amazement, they pulled it off. *Motivational speaking could be my backup career,* Dante swooned to himself. They offered Claudia and her friends a quick tutorial on how to make them so they could recreate the tasty drinks even after the wedding; then they entertained them with their bottle tossing skills. Claudia and her friends ate up the show, loving every second of it, and selecting several cocktails from the made-up menu.

"I'll go check on the main courses," Dante said, hurrying off to the kitchen. With a sigh and palpable urgency in his voice as he turned the corner, he asked, "Any sign of him? How long on the dishes? *I can't stall much longer.*"

"You will have to," was Lucy's only reply.

Taking a deep breath and putting on the biggest smile, Dante headed back to Claudia and her friends. Preparing to make his excuses and stall, Dante was surprised when the kitchen doors swung open and Ben hurried in, pushing a tray with four main course options. The aroma of thyme, rosemary, salmon, and Ramos' signature red wine sauce filled the room, making Dante's stomach rumble and his mouth water.

"Dinner is served," Ben pronounced in his handsome voice.

Dante tried to hide his annoyance. But Ben caught the look and offered him a cheeky smile and a wink in response.

"Miss Herman. I present baked salmon with zucchini and herb salad, and slow-roasted lamb shoulder with my signature secret red wine marinade. Looking at your choices for wine, cocktails, and appetizers, I have also made two more options I think you will love to try. I have ginger and secret herb prawns with roasted rice. Lastly, I have prepared buffalo ricotta and basil zucchini flowers with asparagus and a prosecco dip." Ben smiled, laying the dishes out for the women to try.

"Oh my *god,* these are amazing. I know I had made the right choice picking you," Claudia cheered while all social graces went out the window as she gobbled the wonderful food.

The ladies tucked into Ben's delicious foods, and Dante and Ben excused themselves to prepare for the dessert tasting. Once they were alone in the kitchen, Dante could no longer bite his tongue.

"What time do you call this? Are you *completely* incompetent? You got lucky this time, but if you pull a stunt like this again, I can assure you Love and Joy will *never* work with you again." Dante snapped.

"Relax, Guapo. I got here on time. I was preparing the main course. I knew my team could handle everything else," Ben said plainly while plating a rhubarb and gingerbread truffle.

"You got lucky. If Miss Herman keeps you on for her wedding, I expect you to be *on time* from here on out," Dante insisted.

"Por favor Guapo, don't worry so much; it will give you wrinkles. And you are far too good looking for that," Ben winked, blowing a kiss in Dante's direction.

"Oh please, just do the job we are paying you for, and don't mess this up," Dante rolled his eyes and headed out to Miss Herman and her friends.

Delighted with the selection of foods and how Dante went above and beyond to please her and her friends, Miss Herman left, having picked her final food, drink, and cocktail list for the wedding. She kissed Dante on both cheeks while getting ready to leave.

"Thank you, Dante. Believe me, all our followers will hear about the wonderful job Love and Joy did here today. I am so excited about the big day, talk soon. Adios," Claudia waved.

Finally allowing himself to breathe, Dante headed back inside. Dante emailed the finalised food selection to Ben and Juliette and called Juliette to send the completed contracts over to Ben. Running his hands over his face, Dante sat, taking the weight of his feet that had suddenly begun to ache.

"Here, try this. You look like you need it," Ben offered, handing Dante a cocktail.

"I'm driving," Dante answered.

"It's virgin," Ben replied.

Dante took the drink and choked back at how strong it was.

"That was *not* a virgin cocktail," Dante spluttered.

"I thought you could do with relaxing. You look so tense, Guapo. Take a load off and have a drink with me."

"I don't think so. I will have the contracts for the Herman wedding emailed to your office right away. Do not delay in signing them." Date packed his bag and shrugged on his jacket.

"Whatever you say, Guapo."

"And *stop* calling me Guapo," Dante yelled as he left the room.

Five

EVERYTHING WAS in order for Claudia's wedding. The event was only a few weeks away and the guests had all rsvp'd. The wedding cake design had been finalised, the dresses and suits had been altered, and the venue had accepted the changes and the expanded guest list. Juliette and Dante had received no more late-night calls from Claudia, and all was well.

Avery had arrived back from her honeymoon and took control of the planning, giving Juliette and Dante a few well-deserved days off. Dante travelled out of town to spend some time with his mother, who insisted on his opinions about her wedding, but Dante was adamant he wouldn't help. He had enough issues surrounding marriage because of his mother's past, and he didn't want her to spoil his love of wedding planning. When Avery called, Dante was happy to end his trip early.

"Sorry to ask, but Miss Herman is insisting you help with this as you did so well last time," Avery said.

"It's okay, to be honest, I'm happy for the distraction. What's the problem this time?"

"You are not going to like this, but she wants to arrange another tasting with Ramos," Avery cringed.

"You have *got* to be kidding; we finalised the menu weeks ago," Dante complained.

"I know, apparently another one of her friends needs to give her stamp of approval."

"What is it with this woman and her constant need for her friend's approval? It is her wedding, isn't it?" Dante thought of Ben and how handsome he looked gliding around the kitchen preparing the desserts.

"I know. Do you want me to make the arrangements with Ramos?"

"*Please*. Dealing with him on the day is going to be bad enough," Dante sighed.

"I'll text you the details," Avery laughed, ending the call.

The following day, Dante arrived at the hotel to find Claudia and her friend Michelle already waiting. Taking them inside, Dante knew it would be a difficult day. Michelle appeared to be making all the decisions, and Claudia sat back, saying nothing. Dante worried that everyone else was taking over her wedding. He wanted to talk to Claudia alone, but Michelle was like an annoying gnat who wouldn't leave her side. Things went from bad to worse when Ben and his team still hadn't arrived fifteen minutes after the scheduled arrival time.

"Where is he? Can't you control your staff?" Michelle complained.

"I'm sure it's just traffic; I will call again. I am so sorry for the delay," Dante said, rushing to call Ben, who refused to answer.

Dante kept a close eye on Claudia and Michelle while getting Ben on the phone. They looked deep in conversation, and Michelle grew more and more animated. Dante could sense there was about to be an argument. Finally getting in touch with Lucy, Dante was relieved to find that Ben was on his way and had all the food ready and prepared with him.

"I'm so sorry for the wait, there was a little van trouble delaying Mr. Ramos, but he is on his way. Is there anything else you would like to discuss about the wedding before he arrives?" Dante asked.

"Yes, actually. I don't think you are right for my wedding after all. How hard is it to get a caterer here on time for a tasting? This is not the first time he has been late. Don't think I am stupid. I know you were stalling us last time. If he isn't here in the next ten minutes, I am pulling my wedding from Love and Joy, and I will make sure you never get a booking in Summershore again. I have almost a million social media followers, and my friends have even more. We will destroy you," Claudia snapped.

Looking over at Michelle, Dante could see her smile; she approved of the overreaction. It was apparent these words were hers and not Claudia's.

"With all due respect, Miss Herman, this is a risk you run when choosing one of the most popular and influential caterers. Mr. Ramos is a very busy man. Before we started working with him, did I or did I not suggest another caterer? You insisted on working with him. I will admit his timekeeping does need some work, but as you can see from his social media, he has never disappointed any of his clients," Dante assured, trying his best to control his temper, which boiled with every second.

"Excuse me? She is your client; how dare you talk to her like that!" Michelle snapped.

"He was respectful, Michelle, calm down......she has a point, though. I am your client, it is your job to please me, and I am not pleased right now. Give me one good reason why I shouldn't pull my wedding?" Claudia demanded.

"Because if you pull from Love and Joy at this time, you will not be able to get your wedding organised in time by anyone else. Also, you are in the best hands. Otherwise, you wouldn't have trusted them with your event. And finally, if you fire Love and Joy, I will refuse to cater your wedding, and I can assure you my social media following is much bigger than yours and your friends combined," Ben said evenly.

None of them had noticed when Ben had arrived. A smile started warming Dante's lips as he appreciated Ben stepping in to help. Michelle and Claudia sat back, keeping silent. Dante worried that while Ben meant well, he may have taken it a step too far.

"How about we start again? We at Love and Joy appreciate your business, and we want to make your wedding as beautiful as possible. So, how about we get this tasting underway because I don't know about you, but I am *starving*," Dante joked.

"You're joining the tasting?" Michelle asked with disapproval, "I'm sorry, but are you coming to the wedding?"

"Michelle, shut up, and let's just get this over with. Mr. Ramos, do you have the new vegan menu prepared?" Claudia snapped.

"Ready and waiting, I shall bring it right through," Ben said, bowing his head.

After discussing the menu with Claudia, Ben and Dante found that she was only changing to a vegan menu because of her overbearing friends, and she preferred the original. Ben could see how stressed she was, and Dante worried that she was losing her love of the wedding. Trying to help Claudia with Michelle in the room was proving difficult. She disapproved of everything that wouldn't be her choice and spent most of her time on her phone.

"How about we prepare the three-course meal of your choice for the main wedding party and the other guests receive tasters of the entire selection. That way, your vegan friends are happy, your nonvegan friends do not feel left out, and everyone can try both options if they choose? I can also prepare a buffet for later in the evening," Ben offered.

"That sounds expensive. Are you sure you can afford that?" Michelle tsked.

"I can do it for the same price, and as an apology for my tardiness, I will also include a free dessert bar and silver service performing wait staff. How does that sound?"

"Perfect, thank you, Mr. Ramos, and thank you, Dante," Claudia smiled.

Michelle headed outside, animatedly talking on her phone to a new sponsor for her social media channel, leaving Ben, Dante, and Claudia alone.

"Thank you for being so patient with me. I know I haven't been the easiest bride to deal with. I'm just starting my social media career, and my friends have made it such a success. I've been on relying on them for help. What started as a little advice has run away with itself," Claudia admitted.

It was the first time since meeting Claudia that Dante thought he saw the real her.

"It's fine, dear. That's what I am here for, to help remove some of that stress. So, you just leave all the details to me. I understand you want your friend's help, but remember, this is *your* wedding, not the rest of the world's," Dante smiled. He so loved to help brides enjoy their wedding day. This is where Dante really shined. It was tough for Ben not to notice the sparkle in his eyes.

Six

DANTE PULLED out his laptop and made the amendments to the contracts for Ben and Love and Joy, while Ben cleaned up in the kitchen. After talking with Claudia a little more, Dante relaxed with confidence that the rest of the event would run smoothly.

Ben came back in with plates of food and drinks on a large trolly. Sitting opposite Dante, he watched him with a slight smile, waiting for Dante to finish. Closing his laptop, Dante sighed and relaxed back in his seat, content that his day was over, and he didn't have to worry about anything else until tomorrow.

"Thank you for your help today. I appreciate it. Miss Herman is a huge client for Love and Joy, and with her threats to ruin the business when we have only recently expanded? To say I was stressed is an understatement," Dante grinned.

"It's okay. We small business owners need to stick together. Plus, she was out of line, and you handled yourself pretty well."

"No, that was all *you*. How much will you lose making that extra buffet?"

"Ah, don't worry about it. Not enough to make me lose sleep. Here. Eat," Ben said, serving up some food.

"I'm fine, thank you."

"No. You have been here all day. Eat, relax," Ben smiled, pouring them both a glass of red wine.

The food was delicious, and Dante was thankful for the treat. He never got a chance to enjoy the food samples and had never tried Ben's food before. Each mouthful was packed with flavour, and Dante realised just how talented Ben was. He finally saw why he was so popular, and why Miss Herman made such a fuss about wanting him for her wedding.

"You are very talented. This is ridiculously good," Dante said, cleaning his mouth with one of the cotton napkins.

"Gracias Guapo," Ben grinned. "I have had a passion for cooking since my Abuela taught me how to cook when I was very young. A lot of my recipes I learned from her. It's why my secret marinades and spice lists are kept so secret. I get to share a part of her with everyone I cook for, but her recipes are just something I get to enjoy. Special memories for me, like she is still here."

"That's beautiful," Dante said.

He could see Ben's passion and love for his craft. The more they talked, the more Dante realised why Ben was always late. He preferred to do his cooking in his own kitchen so he could remember his grand-mother. It was so sweet, and it softened Dante's opinion of Ben quite a lot. But there was still a lot about him that Dante couldn't get past, like how Ben talked to his staff and anyone else who chose to work with him. Though his team never seemed to mind. They knew it was just Ben trying to keep the event running smoothly. However, Dante still didn't like it.

"Allow me to help clean up," Dante said, helping clear the table.

"Oh no, it's fine, really," Ben smiled, taking the plates and stacking them on the trolly.

"I insist. It's the least I can do for your help today."

Ben fell quiet, a smile crept across his face. He folded his arms across his chest, and he cocked his head to one side. Dante felt himself blush under Ben's gaze but couldn't stop himself from grinning in return.

"What?"

"If you really want to thank me, you can do something better than washing the dishes. Would you go on a date with me? Por favor?" Ben asked.

Seven

DANTE HAD TOLD Ben he would think about it but kept dodging his calls. He had fun the night of the tasting, more than he would have ever thought. But there were many things he couldn't get past. It wasn't just the way Ben talked to his staff, or the constant lateness and not answering calls; it was his partying. Ben was ten years younger than Dante, and Dante felt too old to be going out partying at every opportunity.

Ben had his good moments. That was undeniable. He frequently sent freshly prepared lunches to Love and Joy, and coffee, and dropped off specialty cakes there himself on occasion. Juliette and Avery slowly became quite fond of Ben and looked forward to his little gift parcels.

"Oh, my days, Dante, your new boyfriend is going to make me fat. This food is too delicious. I can't stop eating," Avery joked, taking another bite of her Tarta de Santiago.

"How many times do I have to tell you? He is *not* my boyfriend. He is just very persistent in wanting a date."

"Have you given him an answer yet?" Juliette asked between bites of bruschetta.

"No," Dante replied.

"Because you like him and are loving the attention? I can't say I blame you. I love all these little treats too," Juliette grinned.

"No......" Dante began but couldn't finish.

Why hadn't he said no officially? Did he like Ben? Truthfully, Dante didn't know how he felt. But now that Juliette had pointed it out, he realised every time Ben turned up and flashed his piercing eyes and perfect smile, Dante's stomach twisted. But that was simply the flattery, right?

"Honestly, I don't know how I feel about him. He is arrogant, constantly late, expects everyone to work on *his* schedule, talks to his team with such anger and frustration, and is a little cocky...."

"But?" Avery said with a mouthful of Victoria sponge cake.

"But the day of the tasting, I saw a new side to him. He jumped to my defence when Claudia went bat crap crazy, and he told me the sweetest story about his grandmother. He is a perfectionist and loves what he does; his passion is intoxicating."

"Sounds familiar," Juliette laughed, pointing in Dante's direction.

"*Excuse me?*" Dante exclaimed in mock surprise.

"You are a perfectionist, and your passion is evident for anyone to see. You sat here for half an hour the morning after Avery's wedding basking in the after-event high." Juliette laughed.

Dante stuck his tongue out teasingly and wrinkled his nose. Juliette had a point; perhaps he wasn't that much different from Ben after all. But was that enough reason to go on a date with him? Was Dante even ready to date again so soon after breaking up with David? Something just didn't feel right, be it Ben or the timing.

"What's the worst that can happen? You go on a date; you're not feeling it; you call it quits. But.... if you like it, you arrange date number two. Who knows, I might be organising your wedding sooner than you think," Avery encouraged.

"I don't know. I'm not feeling that spark, you know? The feeling when the prospect of a first date arises, that rush of endorphins, the butterflies. Surely, that's a sign it's not meant to be," Dante tried to dismiss the thought.

"How will you know if you don't try?" Juliette asked.

"You can't keep leading the guy on Dante. Either call him and arrange a date or call it off. It's unfair to give him false hope, and all this food must be costing him a fortune," Avery said softly.

"Fine, I'll call him," Dante sighed, realising that Avery was right.

Eight

"HOLA GUAPO, it's nice to hear your voice finally. I thought you were avoiding me for a while there," Ben smiled into the phone.

"Hi Ben, if I'm honest, I was avoiding you. I didn't know how I felt about going on a date," Dante began, choosing his words wisely.

"I admire the honesty; it's a hard trait to find in people these days."

"Yes, well, I always say honesty is the best policy. So, about that date?"

"Sure, I'll make the arrangements. When are you free?"

"Most nights after six-thirty."

"Excellent. I'll text you the details."

Ben texted back the following afternoon with the details. He didn't say specifically what he had planned. The message said to meet him at The Golden Coffee Bean at seven Thursday night. Dante tried to dig for more information. He didn't want to dress too casually if Ben had something fancy planned, but he also didn't want to get too dressed up if they were simply going for coffee. Ben found Dante's worrying amusing and kept replying simply with "wear what makes you feel comfortable."

As the date approached, Ben's little gifts of food didn't stop, and Dante slowly began to open up and stop avoiding his messages. The more he talked with Ben, the more he looked forward to spending some time getting to know him. It took a lot for Dante to let his guard down, but somehow Ben was taking the wall down brick by brick with great ease and little effort. And lots of chocolate, where Avery and Juliette were concerned.

Thursday arrived, and Dante brought his date outfit to work with him for Juliette and Avery's stamp of approval. After the shop closed, Dante quickly changed and came out to wolf whistles from the girls.

"You look hot, Papi," Avery smiled, fanning her face.

Since the girls had noticed how Ben constantly called Dante Guapo, they had taken to calling him, Papi. At first, Dante hated it. But soon it grew on him, and he stopped complaining. His outfit was simple yet smart, dark jeans, a crisp white shirt, and a navy-blue blazer. He had been meaning to book an appointment with the eye doctor for weeks, and as his eyes were hurting, he ditched his usual contacts for a pair of light grey framed glasses.

"I hate wearing these things; they make me look so old," Dante complained.

"Not old. Distinguished and handsome!" Juliette smiled.

"Guapo, as Ben says," Avery winked.

For some reason, Dante was more nervous than he expected. Since he had half an hour before he was due to meet Ben, Juliette and Avery stayed behind to have a glass of wine with him to help settle his nerves.

"You will be fine, it's not like it's a blind date, and he is obviously interested in you. If someone had dodged me the way you dodged him, I would have ghosted a long time ago," Juliette said.

"Ghosted?" Avery and Dante asked in unison.

"It's what the kids say, it means.... well, vanished? Acted like a ghost and left," Juliette shrugged.

"Someone is trying to be cool for the kids. Does this have anything to do with Milo's new girlfriend?" Avery asked.

"What, girlfriend?!" Juliette said, suddenly sitting bolt upright in her chair, almost spilling her wine.

Avery and Dante burst out laughing.

"While I would love to stay and chat more about this, I have a date. Ladies, I wish you both a good evening," Dante hugged them both tightly, offering his signature kiss on each cheek and one on the forehead.

"Have fun; we want all the gossip tomorrow," Avery waved.

❧

Ben stood waiting outside, leaning against the wall. The age difference had never been more apparent. Ben wore loose baggy jeans, a dark polo shirt, and a hooded jacket under a thick leather jacket. Suddenly, Dante felt self-conscious.

"Guapo, so good to see you," Ben cheered when he spotted Dante approach, opening his arms up for a hug, which Dante accepted nervously.

"Good to see you too; you look great. So, what's the plan for the evening?" Dante asked.

Ben pushed open the door, holding it open for Dante. Smiling softly, Dante headed inside. *The Golden Coffee Bean* was like he had never seen it before. A circle of sofas had been created in the centre of the room with all the tables and chairs rearranged around it. The lighting had changed to a soft, warm glow, candles centred on each table, and people hurried to their seats.

Taking a seat, one of the baristas, now dressed in a smart shirt and tie, came to take drink orders. Dante had never realised that *The Golden Coffee Bean* served alcohol after six p.m.

"What is all this?" Dante asked.

"What? You work just up the street and don't know about the *Coffee Bean After Dark*?" Ben asked, "Every night, after closing, *The Golden Coffee Bean* hosts a list of events, including open mike night, poetry readings, book launches, etc. I'm really surprised you didn't know since you work in event planning."

"I guess they organise their own events, and I'm so busy planning others I only come here in the morning. I can't believe I never knew this," Dante said in amazement, looking at how even the pictures on the walls had been changed.

Jazz singers playing saxophones, artists at their isles, poets reading their work. Each picture displayed all the people who had performed there in one way or another. Dante noted that he must bring Juliette and Avery there one night soon; it was precisely the type of thing they would enjoy.

"So, what's on the roster for tonight?" Dante asked gratefully, accepting his Chardonnay from the server.

"Poetry readings followed by Saxophone Steve's soft Jazz," Ben answered.

Dante watched in awe as each poet stood up and bore their soul to a room full of strangers. Each person's words touched Dante differently, bringing a tear to his eye. It was a beauty he had never experienced before. He was in a familiar setting under completely new circumstances. He struggled to control himself as each person finished their reading. Everyone clapped gently, but inside, Dante was on his feet, yelling bravo.

"Next tonight, we have a debut poet. Please give a Golden welcome to Mr. Ben Ramos," said the host.

Dante's head spun round in surprise as he watched Ben stride up to the mic in the centre of the room with such confidence and ease.

"Thank you, everyone. The piece I will be reading tonight is called *Abuela tú me hicitie* – Grandmother, you made me," Ben said, standing upright and closing his eyes.

Dante's heart pounded in his chest; he sat in anticipation, waiting, listening to Ben take a few steady breaths behind the microphone.

"*No seria quien soy sin ti.* I wouldn't be who I am without you. You made me who I am, Abuela...."

As Ben drifted into his own world. Speaking his truth, Dante felt the words. As Ben drifted from Spanish to English, Dante didn't need a translator. The emotions translated his words for him. Dante felt a moment of guilt; he had misjudged Ben far too harshly.

"*De Tu Amado Nieto.* From your loving Grandson. *Te Extrano*

Abuela......Thank you," Ben bowed his head and smiled as the room erupted in applause.

"Ben, that was.... *Hermoso*. I will admit you surprised me. I never expected this to be our first date." Dante smiled.

"A good surprise?"

"The best.... when did she pass?" Dante asked gently.

Ben looked over at him, stunned for a moment.

"*Te extrano?* It means I miss you. I'm not fluent, but I know enough."

Ben smiled back, rubbing a nervous hand across the back of his neck. Taking a big gulp of his beer, he sat staring at the bottle for a few moments, the pair ignoring the young girl now taking the mic.

"Five months ago," Ben finally admitted.

"I'm so sorry," Dante reached out and squeezed Ben's hand.

Ben continued to tell Dante how his parents had passed in a car accident when he was young, and his grandmother raised him. She wanted him to be strong and independent, so she taught him how to cook. He juggled maintaining his business and caring for her when she got sick. That's when the last puzzle piece fell into place. All of Ben's lateness and insistence on cooking in his kitchen and not on site, *everything*. It's because he was grieving. Dante felt sick that he had judged Ben before hearing his story. He offered a heartfelt apology, but Ben insisted it was fine.

"I would have done the same. Truth be told, when I first met you, I thought you were a little snobby.... but then, the more I watched you, I saw you were just like me, a perfectionist who wants to make people happy. You do it by planning their events; I do it with food." Ben smiled.

"I guess we are a lot alike," Dante mused.

"I feel like we are being rude," Ben whispered with a wink.

Dante blushed and turned back to watching the poets. Truth be told, he was enjoying listening to them all. Slowly, Ben reached across and took Dante's hand in his. Dante felt his skin prickle at Ben's touch. It was a feeling he hadn't had in the longest time. He liked how his fingers felt in between Ben's and continued to sit smiling, just content to be in his company.

"I had a really lovely time tonight," Dante smiled as they stood outside.

"I did too, so is it too forward of me to ask for a second date? Perhaps dinner?" Ben asked.

"I'd like that," Dante said with a grin.

As Dante waved goodbye to Ben and headed home, he couldn't help but think how Avery and Juliette had both been right. He was so happy he had listened and given Ben a chance.

"Oh my, that's so romantic," Avery gushed as Dante retold the night's events.

"So when is the second date?" Juliette asked.

"Friday, he is cooking me dinner," Dante answered.

Ben and Dante texted, called, and Ben popped into the store a few times throughout the week. Each time, Dante felt his feelings for Ben grow stronger. Every time the doorbell rang, he would pop his head over his computer monitor like a meerkat, hoping to see Ben walk through the door. When he saw Ben's name pop up on his screen, he would feel flushed, and goosebumps would prickle every inch of his skin.

It wasn't until Friday morning that Dante realised he had felt those feelings before. Many years ago, with the only guy Dante had ever gotten close enough to almost marry. Daniel had vowed never to speak to Dante again after calling off their wedding, saying Dante had broken his heart and led him on.

As feelings of guilt that Dante thought he had buried long ago came flooding back to the surface and the clock ticked down to six-thirty, Dante panicked. And instead of heading to Ben's place for their date, he turned off his phone and ran out of town.

Nine

BEN STOPPED SENDING his gifts and stopped contacting Dante. After how successful the first date went, Juliette and Avery were surprised. But unfortunately, Dante neglected to tell them what happened; that he felt he had messed things up by standing Ben up.

As the days passed by, Dante's guilt grew; it was obvious he had upset Ben. And that was the last thing he wanted to do. Dante had become scared of how quickly his feelings for Ben grew and simply freaked out. He kicked himself for it. He was old enough to know better and should have communicated his concerns or called for a rain check. Instead, he chose to run and hide.

"Dante, how much do you love me?" Avery asked, putting on her sweetest face and batting her eyelashes.

Dante pulled his glasses down his nose and looked over at Avery. It had become her thing to ask everyone how much they loved her while mimicking her daughter's best puppy dog look when she needed something. Juliette and Dante feigned irritation when in actual fact, they found it adorable.

"What do you want now?" Dante joked as Avery twiddled her hair between her fingers.

"Bridezilla is on the phone; she wants another tasting of the selected menu with another friend of hers."

"You can't be calling her bridezilla," Juliette protested.

"Well, I don't, to her face," Avery laughed.

Dante stuck out his hand and waited for Avery to hand him the phone. Then, mouthing 'thank you' before bowing and shimmying back over to her desk, Avery handed Dante the phone.

Dante answered, taking a breath, putting on his biggest smile, and taking Claudia off hold.

"Good afternoon, Claudia. How may I help you?" Dante asked.

"My friend Louisa wants to sample the menu. Can you arrange another tasting?"

"Miss Herman, you are aware it is far too late to be making any changes with the wedding being just days away?"

"Excuse me? I get what I want, and you do as you are told. Now arrange the tasting and do what I pay you for. Louisa is a very influential socialite with a huge following; you do not want to piss her off."

"We don't, or you don't?" Dante muttered.

"Sorry, I can't hear you. Are you arranging the tasting?" Claudia snapped.

"Post width, ma'am," Dante ended the call and fired off an email to Ben's assistant.

"Looking forward to seeing Ben again?" Juliette asked.

Dane sighed deeply, "Not really. I kind of stood him up on our second date."

"*What*?" Juliette and Avery squealed in unison.

"How do you 'kind of' stand someone up?" Juliette asked.

"I freaked out and headed to my mother's for the night," Dante answered, cringing behind his computer, waiting for their reaction.

"That's not kind standing him up. Dante, you full-on blew him off," Avery chimed.

"I know, it's bad. The thing is, I actually really like him. It's just.... I don't know... it's complicated."

"Well, it's about to get a whole lot more complicated," Juliette tutted.

To Dante's surprise, Ben and his team had arrived early, and the tasting was ready and waiting for Claudia's arrival. Dante had hoped Ben would be late as usual so he could brace himself and prepare. *Straight into the lion's den, it is then,* he thought.

Dante offered Ben a smile and a wave when he entered the dining hall, but all he received in return was a quick head nod of acknowledgement. The nonchalant gesture made Dante realise he had really messed up. The tasting continued, thankfully, without a hitch and Ben acted as if nothing had happened. Dante began to worry he had indeed hurt Ben's feelings. Ben wasn't acting cold, but he also wasn't his usual flirtatious self, and Dante missed the subtle flirtations of Ben calling him Guapo.

"Thank you for being so accommodating. I haven't been the easiest bride to deal with, and you have gone above and beyond to accommodate my demands. I will make sure to rave about Love and Joy to all my friends and my ever-growing following," Claudia smiled, giving Dante a tight hug.

Her sudden change in character had Dante's head spinning; he never knew what to expect from her. Yet he appreciated her random acts of kindness. Seeing the pressure she was under to be perfect and to live up to her friends' expectations made Dante feel sorry for her. He remembered seeing his mother going through a similar thing with her in-laws on her third wedding. Watching his mother and Claudia experience the joy being sucked out of their wedding made him more determined to get all the details right. He felt for Claudia. If she was experiencing this pressure now, he worried about the state of her marriage; he didn't want history to repeat itself like it had with his mom. Despite her snippiness and occasional unkind remarks, Claudia was a lovely girl under it all.

"Happy to help, dear. I am always here to help you make your day the best it can be. And just remember, it is *your day,*" Dante winked.

Claudia offered him a kiss on each cheek before heading over to thank Ben. Dante busied himself on his laptop while subtly watching Ben and Claudia talk. Ben was smiling, laughing, and being the Ben that

Dante had seen on their first date. He knew what he had to do. He had to apologize and ask for a second chance.

After Claudia left, Ben didn't give Dante a second look before heading into the kitchen. It hurt Dante, but he knew he deserved the cold shoulder. Taking a few moments to pluck up the courage and work on his speech, Dante hurried to finish his notes from the tasting. He emailed everything over to Avery and sent the new menu layout to Claudia to approve. *It's now, or never,* Dante thought, clenching and unclenching his trembling hands.

Opening the door to the kitchen, he peeked inside to see Ben cleaning the countertops alone. Dante didn't know when, but the rest of Ben's team had headed home for the evening. The radio was playing low from the top shelf above the sink, a Spanish radio station that Dante hadn't heard before. The door closing behind him alerted Ben to his presence, but Ben didn't look up to acknowledge Dante's arrival; instead, he headed to the sink and turned up the radio volume. Dante stood, unsure if he should make a move or just take the hint and leave, Ben obviously wasn't interested.

"Are you just going to stand there watching, or will you help me clean up?" Ben finally yelled above the music, reluctantly turning the volume back to a reasonable decibel.

Dante shook off his suit jacket, laying it over a chair behind the door, and rolled up his shirt sleeves. Ben tossed him a cloth and pointed to the stovetop. It didn't take long to find the cleaning products, and the pair worked away in silence except for the low hum of the radio.

The surfaces gleamed to an almost mirror finish. The last pot and pan had been tucked away. There was nothing else to distract them from the elephant in the room that had grown so big it was almost suffocating.

"So, Ben, I...."

"You don't need to say anything. I can take a hint," Ben quipped.

"And what hint do you think I am giving?"

"You are not interested. I should have realised how long it took you to accept my first invitation."

"No, it's not that...." Dante tried to argue, but Ben interrupted.

"I know I can be a little intense, but I like you. If you were not interested, I would have appreciated being told rather than being offered a pity date."

Dante was stunned. Was that really what he thought? That Dante had only agreed out of pity? It was then that Dante knew how deeply he had hurt Ben.

"It was never a pity date. I'm just.... I.... sometimes struggle with dating, especially when I am forced to admit my feelings...."

"What feelings? You stood me up; clearly, you don't feel the same way I do, and that's fine. I'm happy to keep things strictly professional," Ben said, tossing a hand towel in the hamper.

"You are going to make me beg, aren't you?" Dante joked, seeing the glint in Ben's eyes.

"Only if you want to," Ben winked.

"I will admit, at first, I drastically misjudged you. I thought you were arrogant, lazy, your timekeeping was astonishing...."

"Wow, and here I was thinking this was an apology," Ben laughed, folding his arms across his chest.

"I was wrong. I saw that the first time you came to my defence with Claudia and that horrid friend of hers. Then with all your little gestures, I'm stubborn and don't like admitting when I'm wrong, and as I found the more I saw you, I was starting to warm to you. I got scared. Then our first date was.... beautiful, truly the best first date I have ever been on. You opened up and were so vulnerable, and how did I treat that trust? I freaked out and ran." Dane stopped to take a breath.

"Go on," Ben grinned.

"I realised that I really like you, and I have only ever felt such a rush of feelings once before....it didn't end well, and I was...."

"Scared of getting hurt or being the one to do the hurting," Ben shrugged.

"Exactly. I acted like a child and literally ran out of town to my mother."

Ben erupted into laughter, finally stopping when he saw the uncomfortable look on Dante's face.

"I'm sorry, you were saying?"

"I would like to ask you out on a date. If you can trust that I will turn up this time," Dante finally asked.

"Look, I admire your honesty, and thank you for admitting your flaws. But I'm not interested in wasting my time if you are not really into it."

"I am, I really am. Please. I'll even cook... I'm not as good of a cook as you, but I will try," Dante smiled, his eyes pleading for a second chance.

Ben stood contemplating the decision, making Dante wait in agony before he relaxed and smiled back. Then, the beautiful bright smile lit up his face and eyes. That smile made Dante's stomach flip, skin prickle, and pulse race. Of course he wanted to give Dante a second chance. He wanted it more than anything.

"Si, Guapo. I will go on a date with you."

Ten

DANTE HURRIED AROUND FLUFFING CUSHIONS, straightening picture frames, and checking that every wrinkle and crease had been ironed out of the tablecloth he draped over his small kitchen table. He hadn't invited anyone around to his house in the longest time. His home was his sanctuary, his hideaway from the world, and he expressed himself freely in a way that he felt he couldn't anywhere else. To him, inviting someone into his safe haven was as vulnerable as it got.

The large golden sun-shaped clock on the wall seemed to tick louder than usual. It was like it was mocking Dante, screaming at him that Ben would be around any minute, and that it was far too late to cancel. Checking the pristine kitchen, with all his ingredients laid out, his knives in a perfect line, he started to doubt himself. He was about to cook for one of the most talented chefs in Summershore.

What am I doing? I should have cooked prior to him getting here. What if he thinks my chopping technique is laughable? Why didn't I just order out and plate it up, pretending it was mine? Dante fanned himself with a hand towel, suddenly aware of the heat in his home. He hurried to open the small kitchen windows when he saw Ben's Black Mercedes pull up outside.

Running to the long mirror in the hallway, Dante quickly checked his clothes and hair, freezing momentarily when he heard the doorbell ring. He knew he definitely couldn't avoid Ben now because the small window in the door allowed a brief view inside.

"Hi," Dante smiled, stepping aside to allow Ben to come inside.

Ben smiled widely, holding up a bottle of red wine in one hand and a bottle of white in the other.

"I didn't know what you were cooking, so I brought a few options," Ben smiled.

"That's so lovely, thank you, head through that way; the kitchen is just on the right through the living room," Dante said, closing the door.

Dante needed a second to gather himself. Ben looked amazing. He had made an extra effort to look his best, wearing dark chinos, tan loafers, and a pale grey shirt open at the collar. As he walked past Dante, he could smell his cologne, an intoxicating mix of sandalwood, jasmine, and another scent Dante couldn't quite pinpoint.

"Wow, your home is beautiful. I love the colour scheme," Ben admired.

Dante's home was a mix of turquoise, gold, pale blue, and soft greys. A blend of modern decor with subtle hints of antiques. It had taken Dante years to get everything just how he wanted it, but the wait had been worth it. Every morning when he woke, it was like seeing the finished product for the first time. He loved his home and took so much pride in it.

"Thank you. It's my pride and joy. I feel I can truly express myself here."

Ben followed Dante into the kitchen, perching on one of the white leather bar stools at the central kitchen island.

"So, what is on the menu for tonight?" Ben asked, scanning his eyes over the ingredients laid out before him.

"For starters, I have gazpacho, the main course I'm making duck with a pomegranate glaze, and for dessert, espresso and dark chocolate truffles," Dante answered as he slid the duck into the oven – he had the sense to do most of the prep work before Ben arrived.

"And you say you are not a chef," Ben teased. "You didn't have to go to all this trouble for me. I would have been happy with mac n cheese."

Dante practically slammed the oven door shut, turning to Ben, who was holding in a laugh and failing miserably.

"*Who* told you about that?" Dante gasped with hands on his hips.

"Avery, last time I was at Love and Joy," Ben howled.

Dante was famed for making a mess of his mac n cheese dish for a party he hosted once. Not only had he undercooked the pasta, but he hadn't used the correct measurements of anything, making the dish look like cement. Then, to top it off, he had forgotten he was cooking and burnt the whole thing.

"I'm going to kill her," Dante shook his head, pulling out two wine glasses and a corkscrew.

Dante insisted that Ben not help with the cooking. But after several times when Dante almost chopped off a finger or almost burnt himself on the stove, Ben insisted, if for nothing other than Dante's health and safety. Enjoying good food and great wine, conversation flowed smoothly with any bad blood between them well and truly washed away. Ben told Dane more about his family and his business, explaining how he wasn't really the partying type of guy but had to, occasionally, for his clients or for networking. Dante informed Ben about how he started with Love and joy and the company's plans for the future, with Juliette asking him to look into the process and legalities of franchising. So far, it was all hush-hush, Juliette and Dante agreed to let Avery be the first to be offered her own franchise, but they wanted to make sure it was truly a possibility first. Dante briefly touched on his family history but quickly opted for a subject change. Ben, on the other hand, could not be swayed.

"Hold on, I want to hear more about your family," Ben chuckled.

Dante didn't really want to talk about his family because, especially after one too many glasses of wine, he would get too chatty and most likely reveal a little too much about himself and his fear of marriage.

"There is not much to tell. I don't really talk to my dad, I occasionally get a birthday or Christmas card, and I'm not overly close with my mother. Husband number four saw to that."

"Wow, four times. Have you helped plan any of them?" Ben asked, pouring them both another glass.

"God no! I refuse to have anything to do with her weddings. They are a waste of time; she never sticks with the marriage. She just loves the day's fuss, but the novelty wears off, and soon she's onto the next husband. Weddings are beautiful, and I can't tolerate how she treats them." Dante gulped, suddenly seeing the surprise on Ben's face.

"Sorry," Dante apologized.

"Don't be. You have a passion for what you do. It's one of the biggest things we have in common, and I like that," Ben smiled.

Dante returned Ben's smile but continued to say nothing, wanting to leave the subject where it was.

"Is that truly how you feel? That she just loves the idea of a wedding more than marriage?" Ben finally asked.

Dante thought it over for a moment swirling his wine in his glass. If he was honest with himself, he hadn't given it much thought. He had made his judgement based on what he had seen and how he felt about his job. He had never even asked his mother why none of her marriages worked or why she insisted so hard on finding 'the one'.

"I don't know. I have just spent so much time watching my mother and her string of husbands lose themselves trying to make a marriage work that was never going to. Rather than sitting and assessing the problem, she just jumped onto the next one," Dante admitted.

"Have you ever spoken to her about it?"

"No, it's her business, not mine. But watching her go from husband to husband and both sides experiencing the pain and upheaval in their lives just makes me think marriage isn't for me. It seems like far too much work."

Ben stared back, frozen like a statue with a look of bewilderment on his face that startled Dante, making him shift uncomfortably in his seat.

"I'm sorry if this seems a little out of line, but how can you feel like that when you plan weddings for a living?" Ben asked.

"I love the idea of love, and I love the happiness a wedding brings. It brings out the best in people, and there is so much love, joy, and positivity in that day that makes everything else horrible in the world vanish, even if just for a day. So, I love being a part of that. It's not that I don't believe in marriage; I just don't think it is for me."

"Why?" Ben asked.

Dante felt the same feeling of dread stir in him that had his stomach twisting the day of their original second date. This conversation always made him uncomfortable, and he hated admitting his shortcomings to people or feeling like he had to justify himself. He had spent so much of his life hiding who he was and what he loved to make others happy. When he had finally found himself, it had been a freedom he never wanted to lose.

"It's hard to explain...I think, maybe I just don't want that pain when it fails or to lose myself in a relationship."

"So, if you found your person. The one. Would you never change your mind?"

"Honestly? I've never thought about it. I got close once, but it didn't work, so I went back to my old ways. So, you could say I'm stuck in my ways. A product of ageing, I guess." He smiled.

"Do you want to know what I think?"

"Yes."

"A wedding is just the beginning. It is a statement to the world that this person brings out the best in you, and you do the same to them. It's an equal partnership. If you are forced to be someone you are not in a relationship, then it's never going to work. But when you find that one person, a *marriage* is the most beautiful thing in the world. It's a commitment to someone else's happiness and theirs to yours. You want to help each other thrive and find the beauty in a world that can be so dark. It's an adventure."

Ben's statement stuck in Dante's mind for the rest of the evening. It was plain to see that Ben wanted to get married one day. And for the first time in a long time, Dante began to question what it was about marriage he was so scared of. Ben was a much more profound thinker than Dante had expected, and it amazed him because it made him question his own thinking. Maybe marriage wasn't such a bad thing; after all, the way Ben painted the image was so beautiful that Dante began to think that he could one day change his mind. But as always, doubt crept in.

Was it his feelings or his growing infatuation with Ben?

Eleven

"How DID the big date night go?" Juliette asked eagerly.

Dante shrugged but smiled to himself. He hadn't been able to stop thinking about Ben since.

"Not well?" Avery asked, giving Dante a sympathetic look.

Dante shook his head but kept quiet.

"Everything okay?" Juliette asked, turning away from her computer.

"Yeah, it's fine," Dante shrugged, making himself a coffee.

Out of the corner of his eye, he saw Juliette and Avery exchange a worried look. Deciding he didn't want to ask any more questions, he excused himself and headed to his office, closing the door behind him and cracking on with work. No matter how much he tried to keep himself busy, Dante couldn't seem to concentrate. He was starting to really like Ben but didn't want to lead him on. He knew Ben wanted marriage, and Dante still hadn't made up his mind.

He couldn't live with himself if he led the poor guy on but also didn't want to let him go. Slouching in his chair, he ran his hands over his face, conflicted with his feelings. A short soft knock on the door caused him to straighten, waiting for Juliette to walk in.

"You free tonight?" she asked.

"Depends," Dante smiled weakly.

"Mojitos and makeovers? My place? Damian is taking Milo to see a movie, so we have the house to ourselves."

"I don't know," Dante sighed.

"I don't know is not a no," she smiled back.

"You are coming and that final! You are coming if I have to drag you there by that poor excuse for hair you call a beard!" Avery jokingly yelled from the other room.

"Hey! Cheap shot," Dante yelled back, stringing the small goatee, and checking his reflection in his desk's small mirror frame.

"I'll leave you be. We will talk later," Juliette winked, leaving Dante to finally crack on with his to-do list.

Dante finally emerged from his office to find Avery and Juliette waiting with bags full of snacks, drinks, and goodies for the night's festivities. Dante smiled suddenly, feeling so lucky to have such good friends in his life.

"Come on, grumpy pants, get in the car," Avery joked, wrapping an arm around Dante's shoulder.

"Thanks, guys. I think I need a night to let my hair down," Dante grinned.

"Well, don't get too comfortable. I have everything I need in this bag for one of your famous facial scrubs," Juliette raised her bag to highlight her point.

Damian and Milo were already gone by the time everyone got to Juliette's house. A stack of take-out menus lay on the table with three one-hundred-dollar bills. Next to it was a post-it note with the words:

Dinner is on me. Have a great night. D & M xxx

Juliette flicked on the stereo, pumping out classic nineties pop while everyone headed to the bedrooms to get changed into more comfortable clothes. When Dante came downstairs, Juliette was already one step ahead with a pitcher of mojitos waiting and three garnished glasses topped with fun bendy straws in a rainbow of colours and cocktail umbrellas.

"Cheers! To a well-deserved and much overdue get-together," Juliette cheered, raising her glass.

Clicking their glasses, they all took a sip and burst into coughing fits.

"Oh my god, Juliette, are you trying to kill us?" coughed Avery.

"What's wrong?" Juliette stifled a cough, trying to hide her obvious mistake.

"Give it here, my day's woman, you are not supposed to use the entire bottle of gin," teased Dante.

Dante poured out the drinks and started again.

"Here, try this," he said, passing each their new drinks.

"Delicious. A trick you learned from Ben?" Juliette asked, making her eyebrows dance.

"Actually, yes," Dante said, slinking around her and heading to the living room.

That was the gateway to conversation; Dante was all talk once the gin hit him. He felt like a teenager again, gossiping about his latest crush with his besties. Juliette and Avery hung on his every word, listening to Dante tell them how Ben had him feeling and the wonderful conversations they had on their date. Avery and Juliette oohed and awwed when Dante blushed while telling them how Ben had held his hand and showed him the correct way to chop and how he rescued him from almost burning himself. Juliette laughed when Avery defended herself when Dante confronted her about telling Ben the mac and cheese story.

As the night drew on, nails were pained, facial scrubs were done, and hair masks set. They sat cosied up on the sofa in their comfy pj's with their moisturizing sheet masks soaking into their skin on their third pitcher of mojitos when Dante finally felt it was time to confess.

"So, will you tell us why you were bugging out today?" Juliette asked.

Dante took his time before saying it. "He asked my views on marriage, and I said it wasn't for me and how I don't ever want to get married."

Avery and Juliette sat, mouths open and eyes wide, lost for words.

"What? But you love, love. You plan weddings for a living, and you are so good at it," Avery gasped.

"A wedding is just one day, it's everything that comes after that has me concerned. The thing that has me really shaken though, is that.... Ben....in the short time I've actually got to know the real him.... has me questioning everything I ever thought I knew.... It's scary." Dante admitted while fidgeting with the umbrella in his drink.

"You like him a lot, don't you?" Juliette asked.

Dante nodded, his eyes not leaving the swirling ice and mint leaves in his glass.

"That's what worries me. I've watched my mother have whirlwind romances that ended in divorce. I don't want that for me."

"Who says it will?" Avery asked.

Their conversation was interrupted by the pizza delivery guy knocking at the door. Dante was glad for the distraction but felt better for finally opening up to his friends; it felt freeing to no longer carry such a burden alone.

It turned out to be the perfect besties' night. Precisely what all of them needed. As Juliette and Avery danced around the living room, Dante watched with a smile on his face and love in his heart. These girls were all the family he needed. He made a note to make mojito night a regular thing. They didn't do it often enough. Who knew how therapeutic it was to sit around eating food and drinking cocktails with a bit of gossip? They talked, they laughed, and they cried together. It was something they didn't do often enough, only as often as work and life would allow. It had become even harder to get together just the three of them since Juliette and Avery had gotten married, but Dante was grateful for that evening.

Twelve

MOJITO NIGHT HAD BEEN EXACTLY what Dante needed, and the following day when he woke, he called Ben and arranged to meet for lunch. He wanted to be honest with him and not make the same mistake again by letting his feelings get in his way.

"*Guapo, Como Estas?*" Ben cheered, kissing Ben softly on the lips as he arrived at *The Golden Coffee Bean*.

"I'm wonderful. I had mojito night with the girls last night, and it was just what I needed. How long do you have? I would like to talk to you about something."

"Oh no! that sounds bad," Ben worried.

"It's not, I promise."

Dante confessed his concerns to Ben. He didn't want to waste Ben's time if Ben was looking for marriage, and while he was working on his issues, he still had a long way to go. Ben sat listening intently, hanging off Dante's every word, soaking it all in.

"I appreciate your honesty. Yes, I would like to get married one day, but who knows what the future holds? So why restrict ourselves to worrying about what may or may not happen? When you concentrate too much on the fear of how something could go wrong, you miss out on the beauty around you," Ben said, reaching for Dante's hand.

"I know, and I'm working on it...."

"No. Please stop worrying, and let's enjoy discovering each other and what this is."

Taking Ben's words to heart, Dante relaxed and stopped asking himself *what if*. Juliette and Avery commented that they had noticed a substantial positive difference in Dante since he had agreed to just take each day at a time. In addition, Claudia's wedding had gone off without a hitch. She had stuck to her word and left a glowing review on her social media about Love and Joy and Ben's catering services for all her followers to see.

Taking away the pressure of worrying about his discomfort around marriage meant that Dante and Ben were free to let their relationship grow at a pace that made them both happy. It wasn't long before their whirlwind romance led them to stay over at each other's houses so much that Ben eventually decided it was better for him to move into Dante's.

Everything felt so natural and not as scary as Dante had feared. Ben became Dante's muse, and it was reflected in all the little subtle details he added to each event. Ben quit his late-night partying with clients and opted for more intimate cocktail hours, most of which Avery organised. Both Love and Joy and Ben's catering services were thriving. Dante lived for how Ben had him thinking deeper about the world. The poetry night at *The Golden Coffee Bean* became a monthly date night that both looked forward to. And the night that Dante finally got up to speak was the night that Juliette, Damian, Avery, and Sarah had joined them.

That same night, Ben proposed. Dante expected to freak out, panic, and run for the hills. But it was the easiest 'yes' he had ever said.

Thirteen

AVERY KEPT her promise and handled everything for Dante's wedding. After the fantastic job he did with her and Sarah's wedding, she wanted to return the favour. Dante wasn't just her manager; he was one of her closest friends. And she knew how much he loved weddings and wanted to give him one he would never forget.

The night before the wedding, Juliette offered for Dante to stay at her house. Avery and Juliette knew that Dante loved Ben, and they could see how happy they made each other. But after Mojitos and makeovers, they also knew that Dante still had some fears around marriage.

"Hey sweetie, we are heading to bed. Do you need anything?" Juliette asked, popping her head into the spare bedroom.

Dante shook his head in response, looking out the window and twisting his bowtie between his fingers.

"Dante? What's up?" Avery asked.

"Nothing, I'm fine," he replied.

Juliette and Avery came to sit on the bed with him, saying nothing, just being there for support. They knew better than to push Dante; he would clam up, so they sat silently, waiting for him to talk.

"I think I've made a mistake. This is all happening too fast. I'm not ready," Dante sighed.

"What's running through your mind?" Avery asked.

"What if Ben isn't the one? What if the novelty of a new relationship wears off and we find we can't stand each other? What if, a few years down the line, Ben realises he has married an old man and wants someone younger? What if...."

"Calm down, sweetie," Juliette said soothingly, stroking Dante's shoulder.

"What if I end up like my mother? Hooked on the wedding feeling and getting divorced after divorce?"

"The fact that you have worried about that for so long should tell you it's not going to happen. You wouldn't let it happen; that's why you have never married before. But look at you and Ben; you fell so deeply in love that you changed your mind on your terms." Avery reassured him.

"If you truly don't want to do this, we will support you. But don't make up your mind when you're feeling so emotional. Think clearly and then make up your mind," Juliette said.

"I think I need to make one of your famous Pro and Cons lists," Dante grinned weakly.

Juliette headed to the draw-in dresser and pulled out a pad and pen. It wasn't long before Dante saw his pros list was overwhelming, and the only thing on his cons list was his fear.

"Thanks, girls, this helped," Dante grinned.

"You know where we are if you need us," Avery smiled.

Sharing a quick group hug, the girls headed off to bed, leaving Dante to read over his list repeatedly. The words seemed to become sharp and threatening; the room felt like the walls were closing in. Suddenly, Dante felt he couldn't breathe; dashing to the window, he flung it open and took several deep breaths, but it didn't help.

"If I have to make a list, I definitely can't do this," he said to the piece of paper before tossing it on the bed.

Grabbing a small bag of his things, he snuck out of Juliette's house and ran.

Fourteen

DANTE SAT IN THE DARK, hiding from the world. His phone hadn't stopped ringing since the sun came up, but each call went ignored. Finally, after a night of little to no sleep and much debating, he managed to shower, eat, and put on his tuxedo. He had hoped it would spark feelings of excitement. But looking at himself in the mirror, all he saw was a failure.

"Ben will hate me," Dante whispered to the empty room, resting his head in his hands.

"No, I won't, Guapo," replied Ben's smooth voice.

Dante's head shot up so fast he heard his neck click; looking over to the door, Ben was leaning against the door frame. His face hidden in the dark. Dante flicked on his desk lamp, finally inviting some light into the room.

"How did you find me?" Dante asked.

"When Juliette said she couldn't find you this morning and you didn't come home last night, I figured work would be the next best place to look. You love this place, and it always helps you think. What's going on, Guapo? Talk to me."

Dante's eyes brimmed with tears as he watched Ben walk across the room dressed in his crisp white suit to sit opposite him. Talking to Ben was never the issue. It was admitting his own downfalls. Ben didn't push; he didn't look angry or hurt. Instead, his eyes held nothing but love. Dante reiterated his concerns from the night before, repeating them, making his anxiety peak. To try and calm his nerves, he paced back and forth behind his desk.

"It's not that I don't want to marry you. I do...."

"Save that line for later," Ben winked with a cheeky grin.

Dante smiled back at him, finally sitting back down.

"It just this fear of us failing is crippling, and I'm going to walk down that beautiful aisle with all those faces on me, who will all be wondering the same thing. Are they rushing in? Are they going to fail? And the thought makes my throat close up," Dante panted feeling lost for breath.

Ben jumped from his seat and grabbed Dante by the shoulders, his only interest was making sure Dante didn't pass out. When Dante was finally calm, Ben knelt before him, resting his hands on his knees.

"If you think this is too fast, we can cancel. If you have any doubt, we can cancel. Just know I don't need a big wedding to tell the world I'm spending the rest of my life with you. If marriage feels like a cage, we won't do it. I just want to be with you."

"You would do that for me?" Dante gasped.

"Of course. Yes, I love the idea of marriage, but I love the idea of us more. I just wanted you to have a day as special as the days you give to others."

Dante was overwhelmed with gratitude for the sacrifice Ben was willing to make. He was ready to give up his dream to make him happy; it warmed his heart and then sent a jolt of fear and dread through him.

"No, that's exactly it. I don't want you to give up your dream to please me. That's what I feared marriage would do, change us," Dante panicked.

"You are my dream. Not a piece of paper and a ring. I'm in no matter what you decide. You are not getting rid of me that easy. This is your choice."

"You truly love me, don't you?" Dante asked as if it was the first time hearing the words.

"More than anything."

"I want to be with you, and I want to give you your dream, but....Oh no, it's bad luck for us to see each other before the wedding!"

"Is it the big wedding? All that pressure? Because to me, it sounds like you want this marriage."

Dante thought it over; perhaps his fear was routed in the judgement of others, the pressure of building a successful marriage around one big perfect day. A day he tried to get perfect for everyone because his parents' marriage fell apart, even though their wedding day was beautiful. *That's it.* He thought. *I have been wrong this whole time!*

"I think you are right," Dante breathed. *A day can't make or break something so special.*

"Leave it with me," Ben winked.

Ben left Dante's office at Love and Joy, leaving Dante to think over everything Ben had said. With the kind words, and the heart-felt gesture, he considered himself so lucky to have found someone to make him so happy, and he wanted to do the same for Ben.

Running out of his office and into the main storefront, Dante froze. Juliette, Damian, Avery, Sarah, Emma, and Milo were all dressed and waiting. A makeshift altar had been erected in the foyer, and Ben stood talking with an efficient.

"What is all this?" Dante gasped.

"It was supposed to be a surprise," Milo chimed.

"We do not need a huge fancy wedding ceremony. All we need is the love of our closest friends and family and each other. Then, everyone else can wait until the reception to celebrate with us." Ben smiled.

"This is perfect. I can't believe you managed to pull it all off so quickly."

"I said one day I would have the honour of planning your wedding; I always had backup plans," Avery winked.

"Thank you," Dante mouthed.

"So Dante, I ask you again. Will you marry me?" Ben took Dante's hands in his.

"I do," Dante beamed, "Oh wait, I should be saving that line for later," he winked back.

The ceremony was perfect. The world melted away, leaving only Dante and Ben with those they truly loved to share in their perfect magical moment. However, Dante had a surprise for Ben. When it came to the vows, he had written them in Spanish; it was a small gesture, but a gesture that had Ben overwhelmed. As Dante spoke his words, Ben translated for their guests. There wasn't a dry eye in the room.

"It gives me great pleasure. To present Mr. & Mr. Smith-Ramos," said the beaming officiant.

The room erupted in cheers, claps, and confetti poppers being pulled. It wasn't the wedding he had ever imagined for himself, but it was more than he could have ever asked for. It was perfect. Love and Joy had changed his life; it was only fitting that he celebrated the next significant chapter there.

His dream job, his new family, and the love swelled in the room. Love and Joy had brought everything to all of their lives. Damian and Juliette were trying for a baby, and Sarah and Avery had finally received the good news about adopting their son. Dante looked forward to what milestone he and Ben would celebrate next.

"Juliette, you couldn't have named this place anything better. Our lives are bursting with Love and Joy," Dante hugged her.

"I'm just glad I got to see your love and joy for myself. You deserve it so much," she hugged back.

The End.
Did you enjoy *Something Blue*?
Please consider rating it on **Amazon, Bookbub or Goodreads.**

Have you read the Jane and Kennedy Daniels Mysteries?
Join my Newsletter for updates and giveaways!